SHARED DREAMS

J. KATHLEEN CHENEY

Copyright © 2017 by J. Kathleen Cheney

1st Digital Edition, 2017, cover by J. Kathleen Cheney.
(Series design by Kate Marshall Designs)
All rights reserved.

No part of this book may be reproduced in any form or by any electronic or mechanical means, including information storage and retrieval systems, without written permission from the author, except for the use of brief quotations in a book review.

This book is a work of fiction. Names, characters, places, and incidents are the product of the author's imagination or are used fictitiously. Any resemblance to actual events, locales or person, living or dead is coincidental. The author acknowledges the trademarked status and trademark owners of various products referenced in this work of fiction, which have been used without permission. The publication/use of these trademarks, is not authorized, associated with, or sponsored by the trademark owners.

* * *

For more books by J. Kathleen Cheney, please visit her website:
www.jkathleencheney.com

CONTENTS

A Mention of Death 5
Touching the Dead 43
Endings 93

Excerpt from **Dreaming Death** 153
About the Author 167
Other Works by J. Kathleen Cheney 169

A Mention of Death

Chronologically, this is my earliest story from the **Palace of Dreams** world. This takes place a few years before my novel, *Dreaming Death*, when Mikael Lee is a newcomer to the capital city of Noikinos.

A Mention of Death

Somewhere, someone was dead.

Mikael Lee slid into awareness, an ache in his side telling him Death had visited his dreams again. Groaning, he reached back and probed the tender spot left behind by the slide of an unreal knife between his ribs.

"About time," Deborah said from somewhere near the door.

"I'm all right, ma'am." Mikael licked his lips and opened one eye briefly. She had opened the curtains, and eastern light filled his tiny quarters on the second floor of the palace. A stab of pain seared through his head. Flinching, Mikael squeezed his eyes shut again.

"You'd best get dressed and report in," Deborah said in her brisk voice. One of the Lucas Family's infirmarians, she watched over him every time he had one of his dreams. She laid one cool hand against his forehead, a worried expression on her face when he opened one eye a slit. "I want you to come down to the Infirmary and check in with me later this afternoon."

"Yes, ma'am," he promised rashly. He would have to endure dozens of questions later, but right now he wanted her to go away. She had, after a fashion, adopted him when he'd come to the capital a few months before, so he hated to disappoint her. A second later Mikael heard the door shut.

Left alone, he waited a moment for the throbbing in his head to recede. Then he rose from the bed and dragged the curtain shut. Glancing down, Mikael discovered he still wore his black wool uniform from the day before. They must have dumped him on his bunk that way. He undressed and laid his rumpled uniform out for the laundry to clean and press later.

He opened the chest at the foot of his bed, took out his shaving mirror, and pulled the curtain back enough to let in a mere sliver of light. With his left hand, he held the mirror at an awkward angle to see the wound on his back—a livid mark almost two inches long, swollen with blood. It showed purple against his fair skin. A puncture wound, he decided. The knife must have gone straight to the heart.

He definitely didn't want Deborah to see that mark. He didn't want to worry her further. It ached, but would fade away over the course of the morning, leaving only a faint bruise.

Somewhere, someone *else* was dead. Mikael Lee was still alive, and had work to do.

* * *

Mikael found what he was looking for in the section for public notices of the *Seychas Weekly*—a mention of death.

Inserted at the bottom of the column, the letters weren't spaced properly, as if the typesetters had rushed to get the slugs in place during the last moments before going to print. No details, just the bare facts: two soldiers—neither named on the page—found dead in the early hours of the morning. *An accident while sparring,* the paper claimed.

Mikael frowned down at it, surprised. It *was* the right death. He always recognized the death from his dream when he stumbled across it. But he had only dreamed one death in the night...not *two*.

He never remembered much from his death dreams. They faded in those first minutes after waking, like any other dream. He only retained a few vague memories: emotions, impressions of a specific place or an unknown person. The real details—the ones that told him who and where and why—those eluded him. He usually didn't even know the name of the victim. The manner of death, though, he always knew, revealed by the wounds echoed in his own flesh.

His job at the palace included investigating murders within the Family, the private army attached to the Royal House by treaty. The death of army personnel would be under the jurisdiction of their own investigations office. Mikael *had* worked with that office before on a couple of army deaths. His odd talent gave him some useful insights. His superior—the king's brother, Dahar—allowed it since the two offices frequently had cause to work together. Keeping relations friendly, Mikael decided, made his going down there today reasonable.

He stared at the notice in the newspaper a moment longer, then dug a pair of scissors out of his desk and cut it out. He stuffed it in a pocket of his black uniform jacket, smoothed his jacket and sash, and wrote a note for Dahar. He ducked out of the office before Dahar's son could return and talk him out of interfering.

After a brisk walk down from the palace atop its hill overlooking the city of Noikinos, Mikael crossed Army Square. Once inside the administration building, he made his way along the paneled hallways until he reached the door marked *Office for Intelligence and Investigations*.

Ensign Aldassa, a tall, lean man a couple of years older than Mikael himself, occupied one of four desks in the anteroom of the colonel's bustling office. Aldassa had no trouble concentrating on his work. He held up a hand indicating he wanted Mikael to wait while he finished whatever paperwork occupied him. Similar to Mikael's own junior position up at the palace, Aldassa's primary job was to simply do whatever the Colonel Cerradine wanted, so there was no telling what it was.

"Colonel's out," Aldassa said as soon as he raised his eyes. Like Mikael, Aldassa was a man of mixed race—half Anvarrid—but his Larossan mother had left him with far darker coloring than Mikael's Family mother had. Since Aldassa had been raised by the Lucas Family, that meant he'd been orphaned before the age of eight. "Your boss send you?" he asked.

"No," Mikael admitted.

Aldassa raised his eyebrows. "Well?"

"I had a dream last night..." Mikael began.

"Again?" Aldassa didn't bother to hide his annoyance.

The elders of the Lee Family had sent Mikael to the Lucas Family not long after he'd become a nineteen, hoping that the Lucas Family could find a way to tame his dreams. In the first few months after that, he hadn't dreamed, and Mikael had believed, foolishly, that a mere change of location could end his curse. Then his dreams had started again. Over the last couple of months, he'd had *five*, two of which had sent him forth to this office. "I'm afraid so."

"Don't think I want to know," Aldassa said. "What do you need?"

"A couple of men died. I wanted to look at the bodies, if they're in your morgue."

"Interesting," Aldassa said, settling back. "Heard about that. No reason for you *not* to look at them, far as I know, so you can say you have my permission. Sure the doctor down there will be thrilled to see you."

Mikael grimaced and took his leave, crossing the square again to the hospital.

The morgue was in the hospital's basement. The elderly surgeon who acted as the hospital's coroner groaned when he saw Mikael, but agreed to let him view the bodies. He drew back the sheets covering the two corpses, the faint scent of stale blood rising as he did so.

Mikael stared at the two men he revealed, trying to puzzle out why *two* bodies lay there, not just one. Both men were in their twenties, one a couple of years older than the other: brown eyes, brown hair, brown skin, average height. Much like any of a thousand Larossan men in the city.

"It happens sometimes, Mr. Lee," the surgeon explained, as if to a child. "A misstep on the sparring floor or a lost temper."

But people don't usually die. He'd been a melee fighter himself up to a year ago. Then he'd killed someone and lost his love for the melee. It had been a just death; the man had murdered his father, hoping to inherit, and threatened to shoot his own mother. Mikael had saved her life, but in doing so he'd become a killer himself.

He'd been unarmed. He'd only come to ask questions, following up one of his death dreams, but the man had seen Mikael's black Family uniform and panicked. He threatened to kill his mother if Mikael didn't let him go.

Mikael's response hadn't been anything showy, not like the fighting one used in a melee, meant to be seen by an arena full of spectators. He hadn't used a sword or his knife or a pistol. He'd used a chair, forcing the man out a second-floor window of the Vandriyen Palace before the man had time to get off a shot. It had been quick and brutal.

Death is easier than it looks. That was how men ended up on tables like this.

Mikael surveyed the body of the younger man. "Could you turn him so I can see the wound?"

Sighing, the surgeon complied. The corpse had stiffened in its repose, like a board. "I don't know what you're after, son."

Mikael tilted his head to get a better view. The wound looked like a narrow mouth, its lips pulled back. Its placement matched the tender purplish mark on Mikael's own back.

"Very neat," the surgeon noted. "These melee fighters—when they do get into a serious fight, they know exactly how to kill. I'll bet this fellow didn't even have a chance to scream."

No, I didn't. It had been fast and unexpected. Mikael's memory of his death was hazy, but he hadn't feared for his life. It had been a friendly bout, like any other evening.

Staring at himself lying there on the table, stiff and dead, Mikael broke out in a cold sweat. His knees slammed into the hard floor, and chills chased through his body. He spewed up his breakfast on the morgue's tiles.

A hand fisted into the back of his jacket and yanked him to his feet. Mikael stood shivering, pulse fluttering as he felt again the knife slicing in, interrupting his heart in its rhythm.

"Can't you control that?" The surgeon shoved a towel into Mikael's hand and strode away, his annoyance obvious in his brusque manner. "I'll get an orderly to clean that up."

Mikael threw up every time he saw one of his dead bodies. It was too personal. He *was* the victim, at least in his dream, and since he'd started down this strange path of sharing others deaths, he'd died more times than he wanted to contemplate. He wiped at his mouth with the towel, swallowing with a grimace. "How did the other one die?"

The surgeon frowned. "I thought you always knew. They weren't found until this morning, but this one died slow—stabbed in the liver is my guess. The knife lodged in the wound, so he didn't bleed out right away. He bled internally, though. That's the reason for the bloating."

This body didn't bother Mikael in the same way; he'd not been tangled in this man's mind when he died. Mikael examined the wound, a long shallow slice. The tip of the knife might have just reached the organ, most likely fatal. A sloppy attack, though, unlike the efficient thrust that killed the other man.

"Did you know either of them?" the surgeon asked.

When Mikael shook his head, the surgeon supplied names, Varma and Laljidine, both unfamiliar. "Any idea why you dreamed about them?"

Mikael shook his head. This didn't fit the pattern of his dreams. "You said they were melee fighters?"

"Yes."

"Were they on the same team?" Melee fighters worked in teams of three, usually one strong, one fast, and one smart.

"Don't know. You could ask the colonel's aide, Ensign Aldassa. He'd know."

Mikael rolled his eyes. "I'll go back and talk to him. Thank you."

"Next time, bring a bucket," the old man responded in an irritated voice and headed back to his duties among the living.

Mikael made his way back to the colonel's office, wishing Aldassa would learn to be more forthcoming. He dragged a chair over to Aldassa's desk and sat down. "Did you know them?"

"In passing, that's all. Both older than me." Aldassa shifted back in his chair and steepled his fingers together. His dark eyebrows drew together. "Thought you only dreamed when someone was murdered."

Mikael nodded and shrugged. "Always so far."

"Which one did you dream about?" Aldassa asked.

"The younger one, Laljidine. Have you seen the bodies?"

"No need for me to. Coroner ruled it an accident, not murder. No investigation." Aldassa's dark eyes narrowed. "Why not dream about Varma?"

"I have no idea. Would anyone want to murder Laljidine?"

"Other than his wife?"

Mikael could never tell whether Aldassa was serious. "Is

that a joke?"

He held out his hands. "Hard worker, no enemies from what I know. According to *my* wife, though, Laljidine spent every moment of his spare time on the sparring floor. With the summer fair's melee next week..."

Mikael blinked, not having considered the melee as a potential motive before. "Was he a particularly good fighter?"

"Decent. Had a few weak points. Family trained, so better than most Army."

Aldassa had been raised by the Lucas Family as well, and only moved to the Army once he'd completed his mandatory three years of service to the Family. As such, he'd trained from childhood to fight, an advantage average Larossans didn't have. Laljidine would have been the same, then—well-trained. Mikael scratched his cheek absently. "Could he have been murdered for money? Some sort of betting on one of the teams, I mean?"

"Army doesn't allow betting," Aldassa said with a perfectly straight face.

Mikael suspected *that* might be a joke.

"Goes on with fair regularity, though," Aldassa admitted. "I'll ask around, see if anyone knows what's being bet."

"Thanks. Were they on the same team?"

"Believe so. I'll double check." Aldassa put his feet down and sat up. "You going to fight this year? Maybe fill in for one of the Lucas teams? Your chance to get back at the little girl?"

Mikael tried not to cringe. The joke had worn thin. When he was a seventeen, Mikael had come up from Lee province to participate in the winter fair melee. His team had made it to the third and final round, only to be knocked out when Mikael was *killed*. A spectator fell out of the stands and landed right atop him—a little girl. Other fighters took every opportunity to remind him of that humiliating end. "I'm staying away from that arena."

"Probably wise. She might be there again." Aldassa rose, an unsubtle hint that it was time for Mikael to leave. "I'll ask around. Check back with me this afternoon. About six, I think."

That was the best he was going to get from Aldassa. He had no evidence to prove that the death had been anything other than tempers flaring out of control, and no real pull at the army headquarters. If any betting irregularities existed, though, he could count on Aldassa to root them out. The man was a meticulous investigator.

The morning dragged, his heart fluttering every time it recalled it had been stabbed. Even though the coroner had labeled the deaths an accident, the pain served as a reminder that Mikael couldn't just call it an accident and file it away.

* * *

Mikael checked his pocket watch, wondering if he'd mistaken the time. Aldassa wasn't at his desk, nor were most of the others who usually filled the investigations office. He walked back up to the front desk, where a young-looking soldier manned the desk. The colonel's office was the only part of the army that hired females, usually Family-raised children like Aldassa. This girl looked to be pure Larossan, but Mikael guessed she was one of them.

"Is Aldassa around?" he asked. "He asked me to meet him here at six."

The soldier shook her head. "He's probably out at the field house. Do you know where that is, sir?"

Mikael nodded. The field house would be down at the end of the square, a gymnasium of sorts where soldiers trained for hand-to-hand fighting. He thanked the young woman and headed that way. The evening air had cooled a bit, and as much as he would like to take off his black uniform jacket, doing so outside the palace grounds would get him reprimanded. At least his heart seemed to have decided it was still alive, the tremors past now.

The field house felt cool and humid, and the smell of perspiration filled the air. Mikael moved to one side, where benches ran along the edge of the wall. He counted a dozen army personnel moving about each other on the floor. Practice for the upcoming melee, most likely.

Originally intended to display the martial prowess of the Six Families, the melee had evolved into a sport, complete with a convoluted set of rules, field judges and, for the spectators, betting. The army had only begun to field teams for the melee in the last few decades, and even then, comparatively few of them. The Lucas Family hadn't discouraged it, but neither had they encouraged it.

The soldiers in the field house were practicing for the third and final round, hand-to-hand. Mikael watched, trying to recognize faces. Most were indeed from the colonel's office, where Family-raised officers like Aldassa often ended up. The colonel actively recruited them.

Mikael spotted Aldassa then, circling with another soldier. Aldassa feinted with one hand, then caught the other man and threw him over his shoulder. Another soldier approached, and Aldassa engaged the woman. Mikael tried to decide which fighters were Aldassa's team members, finally locating a large man and a smallish woman, identifiable by the numbers pinned to their practice jackets. He'd seen the woman before in the office, recalling her pretty face easily, but hadn't met the man. As others circled, the large man was forced back toward the woman and ending up backing into her and knocking her down. The fighter designated as field judge for the practice session marked her dead. Looking displeased, she got up and walked off the square to the sidelines.

It had been one of Mikael's favorite things as a boy, practicing to fight in the melee. His dreams had changed that. He could never tell when a dream would leave him with a weak heart or achy lungs, unable to withstand the rigors of the melee, and therefore an unreliable team member. He had more reason to sit out the melee than just the threat of a little girl. And to tell the truth, his heart was no longer in it.

The disqualified woman spotted him sitting on the bench. She pulled off her leather helmet and came over to where he waited. "Mr. Lee?"

"I'm sorry. I don't recall your name." As one of only a

handful of Family personnel who ever entered the army square, Mikael expected most people in the colonel's office would know *him*. Unfortunately, he hadn't had the chance to work with many of them.

"Hanna." She shook his hand and then wiped her brow. "Aldassa said you might come by."

"You were knocked out by one of your own team members," Mikael said, reckoning she hadn't seen who stumbled into her.

"Big fellow, no brains?" She loosened her dark hair from its braid, shaking it out to dry off some of the sweat.

"Uh, I suppose so," Mikael said, distracted. He'd developed a penchant for dark hair recently.

She rolled her eyes. "My husband."

"So sorry." Mikael turned his gaze back toward the fighters. The field judges had called an end to the fighting and were breaking things up. Aldassa stopped to give the big man a hand up, and together they came in Mikael's direction.

After tugging off his helmet, Aldassa ruffled his fingers through his hair, leaving it in sweaty spikes. "Take it you've met Hanna?"

"Uh, yes," Mikael said. "Was this where I was supposed to come?"

"Thought it was the best place to ask around. This is Lieutenant Aron Kassannan, by the way."

Mikael shook the big man's hand. Mikael guessed he must be several years older than Aldassa or his wife. "Mikael Lee."

"The one who has dreams?" the man asked.

"That would be me," Mikael said.

The big man turned to Aldassa. "Ask around about what?"

Aldassa gave the other man a dry look. "The bodies in the morgue. He doesn't think it was accidental."

Lieutenant Kassannan gave Mikael a sharp look. "The coroner was wrong?"

Mikael shrugged. "I can't prove anything."

Kassannan puffed out his cheeks, irritation plain on his face. "Lazy bastard. Sooner they get rid of him the better."

Mikael didn't think he should comment on that.

"Aron's a field surgeon," Aldassa said instead.

Mikael wondered how the man's wife could consider that *no brains*. "Ah. Did you turn up anything on the betting?"

"Nothing," Aldassa said. "Wasn't that. I asked around, no one heard of much betting on that team. Probably weren't even going to qualify for the melee, people said."

"What does that leave us with?" Mikael asked.

"Don't know." Aldassa looked at the surgeon. "Can we get in to see the bodies again?"

Kassannan shrugged. "The mortuary service might have already taken them."

"Because the coroner didn't think it was murder?" Mikael asked at the same time that Aldassa asked, "Can you get us in or not?"

"I can try," the surgeon answered.

Kassannan got them into the army's hospital without difficulty. He simply picked up a key from the soldier manning the front desk. Then they all proceeded down to the morgue in the basement of the hospital. The unguarded bodies still lay under their sheets.

"Which one is your victim?" Kassannan asked.

Mikael hoped he didn't cast up his most recent meal this time. "Uh, the younger one—Laljidine."

Kassannan gave Mikael a measuring look. "I hear you're prone to being sick all over the floors in here."

"I'll try not to," Mikael promised. This wasn't the first time to see this, so he should be able to control it.

Kassannan pulled back the sheet and rolled the body over when Mikael asked. It turned easily in his hands, rigor past now.

The man's back had gone livid, mottled and dark, but the knife wound still gaped. Mikael closed his eyes and stepped away, forcing back the nausea.

Kassannan stayed with the body. "Looking at this wound, Mr. Lee, I don't think it could have been an accident."

"Have you seen the other one?" Mikael asked.

"I don't spend a lot of time in the morgue." Kassannan moved to the second table, pulled back the sheet, and studied the body. He touched the edges of the wound and peered at it closely. "Now this could have been an accident. I don't know why the coroner would have called *both* accidental," he added, shaking his head. "The second one could be, but that first body—definitely intentional. I don't know what he was thinking."

"Didn't want the bother," Aldassa offered, confirming Kassannan's earlier statement about the coroner.

Kassannan frowned. "Do you see the same problem I do, Mr. Lee?"

Mikael nodded. "I didn't think about it until I was watching the fighting."

"Our coroner hasn't been in a fight in his life," Kassannan commented and turned to Aldassa. "There's no possibility they could have inflicted these wounds on each other, David."

Leaning against the worktable that ran along the wall, Aldassa raised an eyebrow. "Sure about that? Want to go against the coroner's decision, Aron?"

"I don't see that I have any choice," Kassannan said with a sigh.

"Not even supposed to be here," Aldassa noted.

What are they talking about? Mikael kept his mouth shut. They were helping him.

Kassannan frowned down at the floor, and then glanced at his wife.

She sat on a stool against the wall back by the door, fingering her knife. Without looking up, she said, "Aron, don't disappoint me."

He threw his hands up. "I have to be the one to get in trouble, don't I? It's just because I'm older than you two, isn't it?"

"I'm just an ensign...and you *are* old," his wife said with a wink.

Mikael estimated Kassannan must be nearing thirty. For a melee fighter, that *was* old, but he didn't intend to point that out. "I don't have jurisdiction here," Mikael reminded him instead.

"Fine." Kassannan frowned at the two dead men, then called his wife over to where he stood. He positioned her facing him. "If we were sparring," he asked her, "could you take me in the back while I caught you from the front?"

She considered him, dark eyes narrowed. "Where in the back? I wasn't looking."

"Squeamish?" he teased.

"You'll just pay later, Aron," she warned.

"Can we stay on track?" Aldassa asked, sounding exasperated. "I'd like to get home to my own wife."

Kassannan showed his wife where to hit, and she stepped back, her brow furrowed. "Clean?" she asked.

"Very much so. The knife went in and out neatly."

"I have to do that from the back. If I try to reach around you, it's going to drag on the way out. That's assuming I get it in clean at all."

Mikael walked up behind the much-taller surgeon, wrapped his right arm around the man's throat, and with his left hand jabbed two fingers between his ribs. "This is the way it has to happen."

"And from there?" Aldassa asked.

"I'm already dead," Kassannan said. "Brain is still going, but the heart's stopped. I think..." He twisted and shoved his right hand out, lightly catching her in the abdomen. "This could have been a reflex motion."

"I'm not dead yet, though," Hanna protested, her hands spread as she looked down at her abdomen. "Cut me there and I die in hospital later, but not now. Maybe I'll even live."

"Would you look at your hands?" Mikael asked.

"I would put my hands to the knife," she agreed. "Shock. Then I look down and see the blood."

"Dark blood, on your hands," Mikael said. "What runs through your mind when you see me coming up behind him?"

She frowned, staring down at her unbloodied fingers.

"Are you going to stop choking me soon?" Kassannan asked politely, and Mikael let him go.

"It all depends on whether I'm in on it with you, doesn't it?" Hanna answered finally.

"Does it matter?" Aldassa asked. "Got one murderer out there. Possible accomplice is dead. Can't try him, can we?"

"It's important to his widow," Hanna reminded him.

"I don't think he was in on it," Mikael said.

"Why not?" she asked.

"The expression on his face," Mikael explained. "It was the

last thing I saw when I was dying. I saw his face. He was surprised, maybe a little afraid. The man's reaction—I knew who the killer was just because of that."

"You're not making sense, boy," Kassannan said.

Mikael tried to dig up the correct image in his mind. Random bits of his dreams would pop into his memory, often just when he needed them. And just as often, they *wouldn't.* "I didn't have to turn around and look," he explained. "It was like that for the dead man. Without looking, he *knew* who'd stabbed him, just by the other man's expression. So both of them knew the killer."

Aldassa came forward, separating them. "I'll talk to the colonel," he said. "Aron, you and Hanna go home. I'll make the report."

Kassannan looked ready to argue, but his wife pulled on his arm. "I'm ready to go," she insisted.

Kassannan capitulated, letting his wife lead him out of the morgue.

"Aron's up for a promotion, so he's going to give in this once," Aldassa noted. "He's righteous for justice, you know. Who *am* I looking for, Mikael?"

"Someone they both knew. This is about the melee. The

killer...maybe he wanted to take the victim off the team for some reason. The second death wasn't planned, just an accident."

"Became murder when he didn't haul him to the hospital." Aldassa wore an implacable expression. "Still, no evidence."

"I'm not any good at evidence," Mikael admitted. "I just *know*, but somehow the evidence always turns up. I think we need to talk to..."

"Third member of that team," Aldassa said. "Hungry?"

Mikael stared at him.

"Know a good tavern, fighters go there evenings."

"Should I go back to the palace and change uniforms?" Mikael asked as they walked up the stairs and out of the hospital.

Aldassa shook his head. "How do your dreams work?"

They'd worked together a few times now, but had never discussed this part. "I don't remember much from them," Mikael said, "but when I do need it, whatever's important comes back to me."

"Convenient. Can't ditch you, then."

Mikael nearly laughed at his disgusted tone. "No, you can't. Why don't I know about this place?"

"Outsider, Mr. Lee."

"Of course." His plague in this city—he was an outsider to

everyone.

They walked for a time, deep into the Seychas district, discussing the possible reasons that two fighters might kill each other, until Aldassa directed him toward a white-painted building with a sign that proclaimed its function as a tavern.

The tavern had its main entry next to the offices of the *Seychas Weekly*. Small wonder then that the newspaper had been the only one to print a notice of those two early-morning deaths. It didn't have the look of a Larossan place, without the normal priest-blessed pennants to bring fortune. That told Mikael the owner was either irreligious, or Family-raised like Aldassa. It was busy tavern though, so that lack clearly didn't put off the customers.

The owner—a man of mixed blood like Aldassa—surveyed Mikael's bloody uniform, stained face, and rumpled blond hair. "So, you're Mikael Lee," he said in a worryingly amused tone. "I hear that little girls always fall for you."

Mikael sighed. He would have expected that joke to die out by this time. After all, it had happed two years past now. Clearly he was wrong.

"Drink on the house," the taverner offered jovially. "No one's ever been killed by a little girl before. A great story for years to come."

"I don't ever want to come here again," Mikael whispered to Aldassa under his breath. It didn't matter that there was a good smelling curry cooking somewhere in the back.

"No, you don't." Aldassa took the glass of beer out of Mikael's hand and took a swallow. "You owe me. Going to keep this." The fighters favored the second floor of the tavern, Aldassa told him, where outsiders rarely went. They headed toward the back of the crowded room, Aldassa stopping to speak to a few people on the way.

Mikael drew a few amused glances—with his blondish hair and black uniform, he clearly didn't belong here—and two of the patrons teased him about his girlfriend, so they either recognized him, or they guessed his identity since he was with Aldassa. *This is going to be an endless visit.*

Aldassa finally worked his way to a table in the back of the room, occupied by a lone soldier with white ribbons tied to his uniform sleeve. He had to be the third member of the dead men's team.

The man gazed blearily at Aldassa as he settled on one of the other chairs. "Didn't think the wife let you come here, David," he said.

Mikael didn't comment on the notion of Aldassa being ordered around by his wife. He leaned against the wall instead, hoping to be inconspicuous. Impossible with his black uniform.

"Liana will make an exception for this," Aldassa said, unruffled. "Business. Came looking for you."

"Why?"

Aldassa glanced across at Mikael expectantly. "Would anyone want to get rid of Tobias Laljidine?" Mikael asked then. "Maybe to keep your team from moving up in the rankings?"

The man closed his eyes. "We were hardly ranked at all. We weren't that good."

"Were you good friends?" Aldassa asked. "You and Tobias?"

"Yes. We were all from the same yeargroup," Matias said, "Tobias, Dan, and I."

Mikael sorted that out in his head. Tobias was the *murdered* man. Daniel Varma was the accidental death. Since they were from the same yeargroup, that made it even more unlikely that Tobias had killed Daniel intentionally.

Yeargroup is stronger than blood, it was said. At eight years of age, Family children—along with any orphans taken in that year—were put into their yeargroups, raised together. Those bonds often stayed in effect even after orphans left the

Family.

"Need you to think about this," Aldassa said, leaning closer. "If Tobias had died, but not Dan, what would have happened?"

The man's eyes narrowed and flicked to Mikael before turning back on Aldassa. "It wasn't an accident."

"Maybe not. What would have happened?"

The man lowered his head to the table.

"Give me an answer, Matias," Aldassa said sternly.

The man raised his head, his expression angry. "Dan has...had a brother. He wanted to replace Tobias on our team." He cursed under his breath. "He thought he was better."

Aldassa sat back, looking weary. "What's his name, and where do we find him?"

"Jan Varma," the man said. "He might be here, for all I know. He often is. Try the third floor."

"What's up there?" Mikael asked.

"Sparring floor," Aldassa answered. "Where the bodies were found." He rose, placing a consoling hand on the other man's shoulder. "We're just trying to get to the bottom of the matter, Matias."

The man nodded blearily and dropped his head back on the table. Aldassa walked off, and Mikael followed, heading back to the front of the tavern.

"There's a sparring floor above a tavern?" Mikael asked incredulously, keeping his voice down. "Doesn't that cause problems?"

"Colonel's been trying to get the owner to shut it down," Aldassa whispered back. "Drunks don't fight fair."

Particularly not when armed with knives and swords. "Now I know why your wife won't let you come here."

"My wife *prefers* that I don't come here. I refrain from doing so to please her." Aldassa gave Mikael a stern look, daring him to disagree. He grabbed the taverner's sleeve. "Seen Jan Varma today?"

"You want to give your condolences? Damn shame, I'd say. He went up to three a little while ago."

Aldassa thanked the owner and drew Mikael away from the bar. "Stairwell," he directed. He paused at the doorway of the tavern, looking toward the back of the room, a frown on his serious face.

Mikael went ahead of him, out of the tavern and up the stairs to the third floor where four doors led off the cramped landing. He opened the first door, looking out onto an empty room. It was a large room made from three or four flats with the dividing walls busted out. Gaslights burned, left turned up. Any sign of blood had been scrubbed from the wood floors.

Mikael walked in, feeling an eerie sense of recognition. "This is where I was," Mikael whispered. "When I died, I was here."

"Don't do that," Aldassa said, surveying the room. "It's unnerving. No one up here."

"Where did he go then?" Mikael closed his eyes, trying to recall what fact from his dream needed remembering. He waited, but nothing presented itself—no memory of the victim's, no vivid last thought. "There should be something," he told Aldassa.

"Dead end, Mr. Lee. I'll search his flat tomorrow."

Mikael suddenly recalled sitting on the roof with his teammates, cooling off in the evening breeze after a good bout. "They used to climb onto the roof."

"Matias, too?" Aldassa asked.

"Yes, all three of them together." Mikael glanced over at Aldassa, wondering if he'd noticed the same thing when they'd left the tavern.

Aldassa nodded once. "Better figure out how they got up there, then, or we're going to have another murder on our hands."

Apparently, he *had*; Matias had left his table.

"You don't know how to get on the roof?" Mikael asked.

"Never even been up to three before. I'll go talk to the owner, get him up here. You think." Aldassa jogged back to the stair.

Mikael walked the perimeter of the room, wondering how to get to the roof from here. He glanced out one of the windows, opening out onto the cluttered alleyway below where bins for trash waited for the city's workers. There was no sign of any access to the roof from the alleyway, though.

A narrow ladder—he suddenly recalled that. Mikael dashed back out into the hallway and ran to the fourth door he'd noticed before. When he yanked it open, he saw a ladder going up, the paint on the metal rungs flaking with age.

He clenched his jaw and climbed, heart racing in anxiety. It recalled being stabbed.

At the top of the stair, a trap door stood open. Mikael levered himself out of the shaft and sat on its edge. Like many buildings in the newer parts of the city, this one had a roof that was partially flat. Across that space, two men stood in the wind, white ribbons blowing from their sleeves. Mikael got to his feet and walked slowly in their direction. He wasn't sure of the strength of the flat part of the roof. The two men argued near the back wall of the building.

"He's going to kill me," the other man yelled when he spotted Mikael, his voice panicked.

Mikael guessed from his posture that Matias had a gun. "There's no point to this, Matias. We'll take him to the colonel. Let the army handle this properly."

Mikael heard the safety click off. A sense of foreboding filled him, making his stomach sour.

"You killed your own brother," Matias said, just audible over the wind.

"Tobias stabbed him," the other man protested. "Not me. I never meant for anything to happen to him."

"We've been friends since we were eights, did you know that, little boy? I was closer to him than you ever were."

Varma spread his hands wide. "I was drunk. I didn't mean for that to happen."

"And that excuses killing two men?"

Mikael inched neared. Something underfoot creaked.

"Stop moving," Matias yelled at Mikael without glancing back. "Roof's rotten."

I was afraid of that. He couldn't give up, though. "Don't shoot him, Matias."

"Stay out of this, boy," he answered.

Mikael calculated the distance—six feet between him and the gun. The killer's eyes flicked back in the direction Mikael had come. Aldassa must have found the roof.

Mikael jumped then, wanting to deflect the gun before the grieving man became a killer himself. He caught Matias arm and yanked it back. Matias fell toward him, his weight off-balance. He landed flat on his back on the roof, yanking Mikael to his knees next to him.

Mikael heard creaking beneath them. "Don't move."

Matias froze in place as Aldassa yelled the same words over their heads. Mikael wrestled the gun out of the man's grip and tossed it in Aldassa's direction.

"Jan Varma," Aldassa yelled past him, "I'm arresting you for the murders of Tobias Laljidine and Daniel Varma."

"I didn't kill my brother," Varma insisted.

"You left him to die," Aldassa said. "That's the same thing in my book."

"I thought someone would find him."

"Be still," Mikael hissed at Matias, who'd renewed his struggle.

"He died slow," Aldassa said in a cold voice. "Died here alone, in agony. That what you call being a good brother?"

"I panicked," Varma said with a sobbing sniff. "What was I supposed to do?"

"The right thing," Aldassa said, sounding closer now.

A bit of Tobias Laljidine's memory floated up into Mikael's mind—a remembrance of him, Matias and Daniel sitting up here on the roof talking on a summer night. The wind felt cool after their bout, and they talked about old days. Like he'd sat there himself, Mikael recalled noticing the weak space on the roof's iron railing, intending to remind the owner to have it repaired. Then again, no one else came out on the roof but them, so no rush.

Aldassa walked closer, gun in his hands. Creaking sounded from the roof at every step.

"Watch the railing," Mikael yelled as Varma stepped back, trying to put some distance between himself and Aldassa.

Varma half-turned as his leg made contact with the railing, his eyes going wide. Then the railing gave.

Aldassa jumped for him, but couldn't get a hand on the man before he fell over the edge with a scream. Aldassa landed heavily on the roof. His added weight was all it took.

That portion of the roof collapsed, sending all three of them down with it. Mikael covered his face with his hands as he fell in a chaos of tiles and mildew and plaster. He landed on the floor below atop Matias, who screamed. Aldassa landed atop them, his elbow catching Mikael in the back. The gun went off close to Mikael's ear.

For a moment, Mikael lay there, ears ringing, wondering if he was dead. Then he wondered if either of the others were, which meant he'd lived after all.

Aldassa confirmed his living state by cursing. "You have the worst luck, Mikael Lee."

Mikael mentally checked with his fingers and feet and decided they all worked. "I'm still alive."

"Get off me," Matias ground out. "My leg is broken."

Mikael scrambled away. Aldassa checked the other soldier, agreeing that the man's leg had indeed fractured in the fall.

Mikael went over to the window of the now-naturally lit room. The owner came in, dismayed at the damage to his roof and cursing them all. Mikael kept his distance. He glanced out the window. Then he looked away.

* * *

A doctor up at the army hospital had packed Mikael's nose.

Mikael had accumulated several additional scrapes from the falling debris, and had some painfully tender bruises in places he didn't want to contemplate sharing with the army doctor. No broken bones, though, other than the nose, and he slept well that night, with no dreams to trouble him.

It showed up that morning in the papers, a notice of the death. Terse as those things always were, it merely read that Jan Varma, army private, had died in a fall the previous evening.

Mikael closed his eyes again. He hadn't been sick at the sight of this body. He hadn't dreamed Jan's death, so it wasn't personal at all, even though he'd been there. He managed to keep a cool and unemotional distance, staring down at the corpse lying under the sheet.

Jan Varma had landed amidst the clutter of the alley on the broken pieces of iron railing that fell with him. One rail had driven through his liver. The other pierced his heart.

THE END

Touching the Dead

The first story published from the **Palace of Dreams** world, **Touching the Dead** was my first pro-paying publication. The story came out in the magazine, **Jim Baen's Universe**, in June of 2007, and was later reprinted in **The Best of Jim Baen's Universe, Vol. II.**

This story is our first introduction to Shironne Anjir, the blind girl with a sense of touch so extreme that she nearly starved to death before her mother found ways to get food into her—the skin in the mouth and tongue, after all, is some of the most sensitive on the entire human body—and an ability to sense others emotions. Join her as she learns to use her special talents to solve her first crime…and reveal a killer.

Touching the Dead

The colonel, Shironne decided, must be one of those clever people, the kind who liked to fix things. She could sense him waiting for them there in his office, his curiosity held at bay, but only just.

Her mother took her hand and laid it on the tall back of a chair. Shironne ran her gloved fingers along the wood, straightened her petticoats and sat down. She pulled her braid over her shoulder, well aware that she presented a ragged picture— the blind girl in a child's tunic. More than two years old now, it was too short in the sleeve. Even so, she'd grown accustomed to the feel of it against her over-sensitive skin, and that made the old blue wool tolerable. Her worn attire, though, would look even worse when contrasted with her mother's effortless elegance. The tiny bells on her mother's bracelet tinkled as she settled in a second chair.

"Madam Anjir, Miss Anjir," the colonel said in a deep, sincere voice. "I'm honored to have you here."

Shironne smiled in response, returning his goodwill without thinking. He stood and approached them, his boots crossing a hard floor, only a few steps. She guessed he must be quite tall.

"I'm sorry to trouble you, Colonel . . ." her mother began, sounding official, as a politician's wife should.

"Cerradine," he supplied.

". . . Colonel Cerradine. This is the Investigations Office, isn't it? We've come to inquire about the death of an army gentleman, a Sergeant Merha. The hospital sent us here to talk to you."

"And why would you be making inquiries into this man's death, Madam?"

He didn't walk away, but Shironne thought she heard the movement of his clothes, as if he'd sat down, perhaps on the edge of his desk. She could smell him from there: wool and leather and the oily black smell of a gun. She caught a faint whiff of cologne or soap, something exotic and manly. She didn't recognize it, but liked it much better than the cloying musk her father favored.

"It's me, not her," Shironne told him.

The colonel's attention turned on her then. His interest didn't fall all over her like an exuberant puppy but sat back and observed her like a cat, distant and willing to wait for its prize. "And why would you do that, Miss Anjir?"

"Because I promised my maid Benia I would find out what

happened to him," she admitted, knowing it sounded like a childish whim. "I . . . um, she was upset and she kept asking why someone would kill him, and I promised without thinking, sir."

"It's never a good idea to make rash promises, Miss Anjir," he said with laughter in his tone.

Harder than he knew. With Benia's distress falling all about her like an enveloping wave of water, she'd been carried away. The woman's emotions had overridden her own, stealing her judgment. "I do realize that, sir."

"Hmmm," he said. "Unfortunately, I can't give you that answer yet, ladies. We've only begun to investigate his death. I will, however, send word around to your residence as soon as I do have information." His feet moved away toward the other side of the room.

He felt regretful, Shironne decided, because he couldn't help them. "You misunderstand me, sir. I thought I could help you. Figure out who killed him, I mean."

He didn't dismiss her idea immediately. Instead, the emotions in his mind locked away as calculation took over. A moment passed in silence. "Madam Anjir," he asked then, "do you intend to permit this if I agree?"

Her mother radiated surprise, but quickly tamped it down.

She'd expected the colonel to refuse. "I gave my promise, sir," she said, "but I must ask that this be handled with the utmost discretion. My husband wouldn't wish it known we came here."

"No, I expect not," he said.

Shironne sensed animosity in the colonel's thoughts and wondered if he already knew her father.

"My people will be perfectly discreet, Madam," he said. "Now how did you think to help me, Miss Anjir?"

"I wondered if I might touch the body, sir."

* * *

The colonel walked with her across the level lawn of the Army Square. Her mother had described the square to her when they alighted from their carriage, but Shironne hadn't been able to fix anything in her mind save the location of the army's administration building on one side of the green and the hospital on the other.

She'd heard men calling out in the distance, a drill or a parade. Their voices drew forth a childhood memory of seeing military men in their sharp blue and brown uniforms, parading along the streets of Noikinos with their long rifles on their shoulders. It was an old memory, and she couldn't remember if their trousers were blue with a brown stripe down the side, or the other way around. Perhaps they didn't have a stripe at all. The men were gone now, their drill finished, and only the normal sounds of horses and carriages came from the square.

The colonel led her through the entry doors of the hospital. Shironne knew the scents well, having spent more time in the company of doctors in the last few years than she cared to. They traversed a flight of stairs leading down to the army's morgue.

She tried not to smell the un-circulated air, pressing a gloved finger under her nostrils. The cool room stank of ripeness and chemicals, of bowels emptied and strong soaps, one scent layering over another. *Someone should throw open a few windows and let the wind sweep through*, she thought, and then wondered if the place had any windows to open. Shironne tightened her other hand on the colonel's sleeve, queasiness welling in her stomach.

Male voices protested her presence, and the colonel went to speak with the men, leaving her standing alone. An older-sounding man argued the appropriateness of a young girl seeing such things, which made Shironne want to laugh. The colonel prevailed in the end, and Shironne felt the men's protests, both mental and vocal, fading into the distance, past closing doors.

"There are people who specialize in investigating these things, Miss Anjir," the colonel said from several feet away. "If you want to back out now, I can send for one of them."

"No, sir. I promised." She sensed his concern. He felt curious, but worried for her sake as well. "I . . . um, don't know where the body is."

"Directly ahead of you, a foot or so."

She heard cloth sliding over an unmoving surface. A sudden surge of unpleasant scents accompanied the sound. It was the smell of old blood, like meat gone stale in the summer heat, coppery and —to her confused mind— green.

The colonel stepped away, carefully folding up his worry and training his mind back to observation.

Shironne removed one of her gloves and tucked it into a pocket in the side seam of her tunic. With the other hand, she reached out and located the edge of the table. Wood, she thought. Her cotton gloves never completely blocked her impressions. She touched a bare finger to the table, sensing things that had crossed it in the last few days, the fluids a body made. There were tiny bits of skin from many people ground into the table's surface, and harsh chemicals. She recognized carbolic acid, long since faded past usefulness. Other things she didn't recognize, or recognized but didn't have names for.

She gritted her teeth and stretched out a hand. It contacted something cool— skin chilled to the temperature of the room. The body remained calm, unmoving despite the seething life that went on inside the dead shell. Shironne grimaced.

The colonel's hands touched her sleeves then, drawing her away.

"No," she insisted, and his hands relented. His worry wrapped around her like a fog and just as quickly fled, hidden back in some corner of his mind.

Shironne laid her palm where her finger had touched—an arm, the muscles exhausted as if the man had recently fought. She ran her fingertips along it, feeling for the hand at its end.

"His hands have been cleaned," she said, sensing soap on the man's skin.

"The mortuary service would have washed the body."

She felt the fingers, finding faint traces of ink, of food, of other things, under the film of the soap. "If he had a gun, sir, I don't think he fired it."

"Why not?" The colonel's mind didn't reflect doubt, only

curiosity.

"There's no . . . um, evidence of the gun being fired. There's something left when someone does that, but I don't know what to call it, though." She'd only ever touched a gun once before, and had no names for those things beyond gun and bullet.

The colonel's fascination grew. "We haven't found his pistol, I believe."

Shironne ran her fingers back up the arm and touched the dead man's chest. She found the edge of a wound and forced her senses deeper. A knife, tearing through the skin and into the heart, ruining its rhythm— a knife killed him. She could almost picture the blade in her mind. "Do you have the knife?"

"No, the killer took it. We hope he still has it."

"It should be long and narrow. If you find it, I can tell you if it's the one, I think."

"By touching it?"

"Yes, sir. It would have his blood on it, and I would recognize his blood now, sir." She had no words to explain that either.

"If I'd stabbed someone, I'd clean the knife," he pointed out.

"But it's hard to get everything off, sir. There might be little bits of blood left, maybe so small you can't see them, but I would be able to feel them."

Shironne touched her hand to the sergeant's cold, unshaven jaw, sensing the first stages of bruising there. She'd felt it on her mother's skin before, when a bruise hadn't yet had a chance to swell, the blood vessels all broken and angry under the skin. She suspected the colonel had seen the mark on the man's face.

She took a deep breath and forced herself to feel past the flesh. Memories lingered in the dead man's mind, not fluttering about crying for attention as a living person's would but lying about like leaves scattered in the fall. They were rotting, gone skeletal. She remembered holding a moldered leaf as a little girl and gazing at its delicate framework, back in the days before her eyes had gone sightless.

She dug into the sergeant's tattered memories. His mind held on to brief images: childhood recollections, scattered smells. There were faint snatches of her maid, Benia, in that chaos, different from what Shironne knew of the woman: the smell of her skin, the turn of her ankle, the curve of her back as her hair fell black against it.

Startled by the strange perspective, Shironne shook her head, trying to clear it. She lifted her hand from the body's chilly brow, keeping it well away from her clothes. "I don't think I'll find out anything else, sir. Is there someplace I can wash?"

The colonel turned her about, hands on her shoulders. "Straight ahead about ten feet there's a sink. Can you find that?"

She put her gloved hand out in front of her and stepped off the distance. She found the edge of the sink and ran her fingers around it. Then she stripped off her second glove, located a lump of lye soap and turned on the tap. The soap's slick feel made her want to grind her teeth, but she bore it. Once convinced her hands were sufficiently clean, she worked her gloves back on.

The colonel thought curiosity at her. "How long have you been blind?"

Shironne turned toward the sound of his voice. "About a year and a half, sir. Since I was thirteen."

"I've never known anyone blind before," the colonel said. "You seem quite self-sufficient."

"My mother is very insistent." Her father would want her out of the house the moment she came of age at seventeen. Legally, her mother had no means to forestall her expulsion.

"You also seem quite determined to carry on with this investigation, Miss Anjir, despite your mother's . . . lack of enthusiasm."

Lack of enthusiasm didn't begin to describe her mother's sentiments. Mama had been brought up very properly, taught that a girl should learn to manage her husband's household, bear his children, and follow his commands in all things. Shironne, on the other hand, knew she wouldn't catch a husband —not now— so none of those imperatives mattered for her any more. "She's very reserved, Colonel," Shironne said, "but Mama says that I'm, um . . . the interfering sort."

She sensed his amusement. He let her feel it, as if he held it out on a platter for her mind to see. "You're very good at controlling your emotions, sir."

"I was well trained," the colonel answered. "You must be very sensitive."

"Yes, sir, far more so than my mother." At first, her skin had felt so raw that every breath, every touch, every morsel of food had all been agony in the overwhelming flood of sensation sweeping through her. Her father's very presence had been a torment, his ever-present anger rousing in her a screaming fury of her own. He still made her teeth hurt, even now.

"So your mother's a sensitive as well," the colonel said. "I should have expected that."

Shironne frowned. She'd revealed a secret her mother wouldn't want exposed. "She . . . no one . . ."

"I know who your mother is, Miss Anjir. I would never say

or do anything to harm her."

He meant his words sincerely. Shironne sensed it.

"Why don't I take you back to the office now?" He put a hand under her elbow, guiding her toward the stairs.

"What do you mean, you know who my mother is?" She tried to judge his mind through the muted contact of his hand on her sleeve.

"Hmm. An alderman's wife," he stated correctly.

But his original statement had nothing to do with her father, she could tell. "No, you meant something else."

His mind turned quickly, making inferences from her words, tying them back to what he'd seen in the morgue. His hand slipped away from her elbow, taking with it her tie to his thoughts, leaving her access to his emotions alone.

"Amazing," the colonel said, with no hint of offense. "You don't actually have to be touching my skin."

Shironne wondered what he used for reference. "Should I?"

"Do you not know what you are?" Wonder floated through his emotions, not hidden this time.

"A freak," she whispered. "Witch-blood." They told stories of people like her kept caged in a foreign palace— a menagerie, only not filled with beasts. She had read such stories with appalling relish as a little girl, never suspecting then she might someday belong in one of those cages herself.

The colonel laughed. "Ah, no. Come with me, Miss Anjir. Your mother and I need to have a discussion."

He returned his hand to her elbow, guiding her up the last steps and out of the hospital. The cool fall breeze felt clean after the fetid air of the morgue, even if it did brush her cheeks with a touch of factory smoke.

Her mother waited in the colonel's office, anxiety spinning about her in a tight skein. "Are you all right, sweetheart?" she asked as they came through the door.

Shironne wished she could put her arms around her and be held for a moment, but Mama was a politician's wife and had to keep up her cultured image. "I'm fine, Mama. It was . . . unpleasant, but I'm fine."

Her mother tucked away her fretfulness. She reached out and plucked a stray bit of hair away from Shironne's face, the sound of her bracelet warning Shironne first. Unlike her mother's, Shironne's hair was curly, constantly going astray despite her braid. "Did you find out what you needed?"

"No. I . . ." Shironne turned in the colonel's direction, a sudden inspiration electrifying her. "Can you take me to where he lived?"

"Sweetheart," her mother protested, discomfited. "I'm certain the colonel has other . . ."

"I promised, Mama. I told Benia I would find out why."

"Madam Anjir," the colonel said in a grave voice, "I'm willing to take her there. I am curious."

Her mother flinched at his last word. Shironne felt it both through Mama's tight grasp on her hand and in her sudden air of anger. "My daughter is not a circus freak, Colonel Cerradine. She didn't come here to entertain you."

"No, Madam, she came to fulfill a promise, and I intend to help her do so." The colonel radiated honesty, so clearly that Shironne wondered if he practiced at home.

"Colonel, my husband doesn't want her seen . . ."

"Is he the one who first used the word 'freak,' Madam?" the colonel asked in an irritated voice. "The proper term is touch-sensitive."

Silence reigned for a moment.

Shironne felt fear tumbling through her mother's heart. The emotion reflected through her own body, sending goose bumps shivering along her arms. A trickle of perspiration ran down her back. Shironne fought the response, trying to keep it from taking over her own thoughts. "What do you mean, Colonel?"

"If I'm not mistaken, Miss Anjir, you are a rare form of sensitive, much more acute than most. The talent does run in certain families."

The colonel waited for her mother to admit something. When he got no response, he continued. "I was raised at the Fortress, Madam, as were many of my staff. We don't view such things as most people do. We're a little more open-minded."

Beneath the palace that housed the king and his household lay the Fortress, home to the Lucas Family—the king's protectors who were known to possess the ability to sense others' intentions. Through its relationship with the Lucas Family, it was often claimed that the king's relatives possessed those same "talents."

Her mother didn't respond to the colonel's statement.

"The prince is one of my closest friends," he tried again. "I would never harm a member of his family."

Shironne decided he'd approached the topic so obliquely because he feared Mama had never admitted it to her. He didn't wish to expose Mama's secret.

"I . . . um," her mother faltered, ". . . my husband . . ."

"Doesn't want anyone to know," the colonel finished. "I

understand. I can see he asks you to keep many secrets." A distinct flash of anger accompanied those words.

Clearly, the cosmetics Mama used to hide the new bruise hadn't fooled him. Shironne sensed her mother's fleeting humiliation.

She knew the expression Mama would be wearing now. She'd seen it often as a little girl. Savelle Anjir was tall, beautiful, and elegant, always cloaked in the mantle of the serene politician's wife. Only after her odd sensitivity developed had Shironne begun to understand that her mother's cool tranquility was a facade.

"He is my husband, Colonel," Mama insisted with a quaver in her voice. "He may ask what he wills."

"Why not go to your brothers for protection?"

Officially, her mother had no brothers. "That is not your concern, Colonel," she said more firmly.

Shironne sensed his frustration, but her mother would never give in to his gentle and well-intentioned suggestions. It would cause a scandal. Shironne spoke into the stretching silence. "Colonel, do you think I might go to his apartments?"

"I will accompany you there shortly," the colonel answered, "if your mother permits."

"Her father . . ."

"Would not want her seen. I recall, Madam. Let me go talk to Lieutenant Kassannan. I'll see if she can't come up with something and accompany us there." He walked out of the room, leaving the two of them alone.

Being exposed as the old king's bastard had always been Mama's greatest fear. While the king and the prince might be her half-brothers, she had never met them...even though she sometimes half-wished for it.

"He won't say anything, Mama. I can tell," Shironne assured her.

Her mother sighed. "We need to get home, sweetheart. We don't have the time to go visit this man's rooms."

The butler always snitched to Father if Mama left the house for too long. Father paid him well. "You could go back, Mama."

"And leave you here alone?" Her voice sounded incredulous.

"I'll be safe with the colonel. I can tell. If you go back, the butler probably won't even notice I didn't come in. He never notices me. I'll come back as soon as I'm done and I'll make certain he doesn't see me. Cook won't say anything." Her mother still didn't like the idea— Shironne could sense her worry. "I gave my word, Mama. I must."

Her mother understood duty all too well. She sighed again and finally agreed to the plan, unhappily so.

The colonel returned then, seeming pleased with himself. His step even sounded lighter. "Why don't you put this on, Miss Anjir?"

He handed her something. Shironne turned it about in her gloved hands, determining she held a woman's hat. She righted it and placed it on her head.

"There's a veil." He folded it down over her face.

Judging by her mother's smothered laughter, she must look ridiculous. The hat tilted, dipping down over her face. Its headband came into contact with her forehead, hinting at the woman who'd worn it before, an aged deposit of oils, dirt, and skin.

"It's a little large," the colonel observed.

Her mother tucked away her amusement, deciding to be firm again. "Colonel, I will let you take her, but I must return to my house. Could you possibly send her back there— with a suitable escort, of course?"

"Of course, Madam Anjir."

* * *

"Are you really in the Army?" Shironne asked the woman who led her down the steps of the administration building—Lieutenant Kassannan. Realizing she'd been rude, she put her hand over her mouth only to tangle her fingers in the veil of the over-large hat.

"Yes, miss," the lieutenant said, not sounding the least offended. "The Investigations Office does take on female workers."

Shironne wondered if she heard that question often. She'd known there were women who served in the Army, but had never thought to meet one. Clearly, the colonel considered women competent to do something other than run a household. "Do you enjoy it?" she asked.

"Yes, miss," the lieutenant said. "It's my calling, I think. I am good at what I do."

The colonel joined them, his boots ringing on the steps. Shironne heard a carriage driving up, the horses' hooves closer than she'd expected. Lieutenant Kassannan helped her up and then sat next to her, her mind as politely disciplined as the colonel's.

"I knew about my mother's birth," Shironne told the colonel after they started on their way, "but she doesn't like to talk about it."

"I suspect your mother's friends would be shocked if they learned of it," he said guardedly.

The carriage had a smooth ride, far better than the aging one her family owned. "My mother doesn't really have any friends," Shironne said. "Father doesn't like for her to meet people."

That made the colonel angry. The lieutenant's mind reflected suspicion as well.

"I mean, she meets people at political things," Shironne amended, "just not on her own." Father preferred to keep his beautiful and purportedly well-born wife close.

"Hmm," the colonel said.

The carriage began slowing. They'd traveled only a short distance, so she knew they'd stayed in the same district of the city. The colonel straightened her hat's veil. "Are you ready?"

"Do I look as ridiculous as my mother thought?" A heavy scarf might have worked better than this hat, but she supposed he simply hadn't had one close at hand.

"Yes," the colonel answered. The lieutenant laughed and agreed as they rolled to a stop.

The colonel handed her down from the carriage onto a

cobbled street. Other traffic passed by, but not much. The factories smelled nearer than before. Trees rustled in the faint breeze. The veil confused her, brushing into her face, startling her skin with the feel of silk lace and dye.

She heard the lieutenant jump down from the carriage, her booted feet striking the cobbles. From the sounds she made, Shironne deduced that Lieutenant Kassannan must wear trousers just as the colonel did, but no petticoats.

"Why don't we go in?" the colonel asked. He took Shironne's gloved hand and laid it on his sleeve, leading her up a few steps and into the entryway of a house.

Home-smells surrounded Shironne, and the taste of dirt. The owner didn't keep it as clean as her house. "Is this his house?"

"It's a boarding house," the colonel explained. "He had a flat here. I sent a message ahead, to let the landlady know we were coming back."

"Oh." She should have realized that. A sergeant wouldn't have the money to own a house. In fact, Benia claimed that as the reason they hadn't married yet.

Voices echoed along hallways, distracting her. Late morning, and most of the residents should be at their work, Shironne guessed. Not all, it seemed. Two women argued somewhere above them, one angry, another pleading, their words indistinct at this distance.

"Upstairs, sir," the lieutenant said.

The colonel drew Shironne toward the sounds of the voices and they mounted the stairs. Someone passed close by as they came out onto the second-floor landing, causing the colonel to halt abruptly. She hummed a lullaby under her breath, a fog of vague despondency surrounding her.

"I beg your pardon, Madam," the colonel said, even though she'd been the one to walk into him.

The woman's attention focused on him, her sudden interest pronounced enough to make Shironne wonder for the first time if the colonel was a handsome man. Then the woman's attention drifted away like smoke caught on the wind. Without even responding, she continued up the stairs.

The landlady, identifiable by the keys jangling from her wrist, met them when they stopped at a doorway. She fawned over the officers in a subservient fashion and unlocked the door for them, curious and uneasy thoughts making a messy cloud around her in Shironne's mind. The colonel thanked her and informed her they would send for her if they needed further assistance— a polite way of asking her to go away. She left them, taking her worry and noisy keys with her.

Shironne laid a gloved hand on the doorframe and stepped through onto a wood floor. "How is the room laid out?"

The colonel entered behind her, giving her a brief description. The sitting room possessed only a low table, two chairs and a tea service near the hearth.

"Could you take me to a chair?" Shironne asked.

He took her hand, curiosity in his mind again, and placed it on the back of a chair. She sat and removed her left boot. "Is there anything on the floor?"

"A braided rug in front of the hearth."

Shironne stood and started away from the chair, feeling about with her bared foot. She couldn't sense much from the wood itself, but wood kept things. She felt dirt trapped in the grain, bits of skin and hair, food and spices and saliva, all ground together into dust, only faintly identifiable. The pine floors had recently been scrubbed with lye and water.

Shironne reached a spot near the middle of the room and stopped, her foot poised barely touching the floor. Blood had flowed there. "Did he die right here?"

"That was where they found the body this morning," the lieutenant confirmed from just inside the doorway.

"There's a lot of blood."

"I don't see anything," the colonel said. "The landlady must have scrubbed it after they took the body."

"But she didn't get it all. You never get anything really clean, sir. I can feel the blood in the cracks between the boards, and in the grain of the wood."

"Hmmm. Are your feet as sensitive as your hands?"

"No, sir, but more than . . . um, say, my elbow."

"Interesting."

Shironne moved her foot about, tapping spots on the bare wood. The blood had spread wide, which made her suspect the body laid there for some time. "How long before anyone found him, sir?"

"We don't know for certain. They found the body early this morning and carried it to the morgue at about seven."

She began making a wider circle, trying to determine what else the floor could tell her. "Someone barefoot was here, someone with small, dirty feet. They got some of the blood on them and probably left footprints."

"Gone now. A child or a woman?"

"Female, but definitely not my maid. Benia never goes barefoot. Once I told her what was really on the floor," Shironne almost laughed, remembering the woman's unseen horror, "and now she can't do it anymore."

She continued feeling her way outward. She crossed a spot where many shod feet had passed, leaving dirt from the street outside. She came to a halt and pointed in the direction of the traffic. "What's that way, sir?"

"Bedroom," he said.

She followed the track the feet had walked.

"There's a closed door about three feet in front of you," the colonel warned her.

Shironne reached out a hand and located the door. She slid off one of her gloves and touched the porcelain doorknob. "The landlady cleaned this, too."

"She'll want to let these rooms again quickly."

"That doesn't help me much."

"I don't think she had you in mind."

Shironne turned the knob and pulled the door open. The bedroom smelled stale, as if air didn't pass through it. "Is there no window?"

"No," the colonel replied from close behind her. "It's a tiny room, only the bed and an armoire. Hardly space to turn around."

She stepped into the room, unexpectedly cracking her shin

on a metal bed frame on her first step. She hissed, tears starting in her useless eyes.

"I'm sorry," he said. "I should have warned you."

"Not your fault, sir," she said, regaining her equilibrium. She hated doing things like that— things people expected a blind girl to do.

She leaned down and touched the bedclothes, feeling wool, worn and coated with years of human use. They'd been washed recently, but soap never got rid of everything. "The landlady must have re-made the bed."

Frustrated, she reached out her gloved hand and tugged back the blanket, exposing the sheets. She pulled back the upper one, hoping not to dislodge the lower sheet at the same time.

"I don't believe your mother would approve of this," the colonel said, his mind abruptly focused on her actions.

"She's not here," Shironne reminded him. She ran her bare hand lightly across the sheet, starting at the head of the bed. "The landlady may have made the bed," she told the colonel, "but she didn't change the sheets."

The colonel radiated disgust.

"The sheets—they feel of him, the same man who bled on the floor."

"How can you tell?"

"I . . . um, don't know how, sir. I just know. Different people just feel different to me. I don't have any words for it. I recognized his blood because I'd touched his body. I recognize the sheets for the same reason, but I can't explain how."

"The sheets?"

"Um . . . what's on the sheets, sir. People leave bits of themselves behind; hair, skin, spit . . . other things." She slid her hand farther down the sheets and stopped. "I can feel him here," she said, "and . . . um, also my maid, Benia."

Embarrassment bloomed around him. "I think perhaps we've seen enough."

Shironne almost laughed at his sudden squeamishness. "Colonel, I've touched this sort of thing before. I've known for some time my maid had a lover. Perhaps you shouldn't mention that to my mother, though."

He packed away his worry and sighed. "You are a most unusual young lady."

"Thank you, sir. It's just . . . I mean, how can I miss that sort of thing?" The world never stopped for her too-sensitive skin. "The odd thing is, another woman had been in this bed. The barefoot one, I think, although I'm not certain. I didn't really get much of a feel of her from the floor."

"Ah. I'm sorry for your maid, then," the colonel said with a hint of sympathy followed by a quick flare of suspicion.

"Benia wouldn't do this, sir. She loved him."

"People sometimes do irrational things when wounded."

"But she couldn't have lied to me about it, sir. People can't fool me if I'm touching them."

That revelation sparked another fit of cogitation on his part, so Shironne returned her attention to the sheets. "Sir, I don't think the barefoot woman was his lover, or at least . . . um, not since these sheets were washed."

"Hmm." He worried again.

"I mean, I can feel a lot of him on the sheets, and a lot of Benia, but only hints of the other woman. I mean, if she was his lover too, there would be more . . ." She stopped, not certain how to explain it.

"There would be more," he said firmly, sparing her.

"Yes, sir."

"So another woman was here," he said. "There could have been a fight over her."

"And perhaps her husband killed the sergeant?"

"It would make sense," the colonel said. "At least now we

have a possible motive to follow up on."

"I really don't think he would have brought another woman here, sir. He loved Benia."

"No, you know she loved him. Can you be certain he felt the same?"

Shironne dug back through her own memories, trying to recall everything Benia had ever said of her sergeant. "I just can't believe it, sir."

The colonel thought cynical thoughts. "You're very young. You want to believe the best of others."

"I'm fourteen," she told him, wondering if he could possibly know the evil in others' minds the way she did. "Is there anything else here I could feel, sir?"

She heard him move past her into the small room. He opened the armoire and then shut it. "The landlady has removed everything already. Lieutenant?" he called back to the main room.

"Yes, sir," the woman replied promptly.

"Find out what the landlady did with the sergeant's personal property." The lieutenant agreed and left, her quiet presence fading away with her footsteps. "I think we know now why she looked nervous."

Shironne followed her own trail back to the chair she'd sat in and felt around to retrieve her shoe. She finally located it and pulled on her sock. She was tying her shoe when the colonel came to tower over her.

"I believe we're at a dead end for now," the colonel said. He touched a hand to her shoulder. "I should get you back to your house before your father misses you."

Anger flared through his thoughts again.

"He doesn't watch me as close as Mama."

He took his hand away. "Still, I suspect he might blame her if he knew you were missing, wouldn't he?"

"Yes, sir." She'd already chanced her father's ire by being gone this long.

"Why don't I take you back then?" he said. His tone didn't indicate a question.

Shironne sighed and rose. "I need to know, though, when you find out who did it."

"I'll get you word. I promise."

* * *

The butler believed Mama's fabrication about locking

Shironne in her room for the entire afternoon. When he found Shironne below stairs chatting with Cook in the kitchens, he roundly upbraided the woman for abetting her delinquency. The butler would prefer she be locked away permanently, Shironne knew. He feared her "oddness" might be catching.

She put a tearful Benia off with the assurance that the colonel would keep them informed, feeling horribly guilty the whole time.

"I hope he finds out who did it," Shironne said that night while her mother brushed out her hair. Her father hadn't returned home for some reason, the best possible end to any day. "Benia seems like she'll never be happy again."

"I know. I sense it too. Did he say he would let us know what he found?"

Trepidation accompanied her mother's question, coupled with a hint of anticipation. Mama apparently had mixed feelings about the colonel and his inquisitive nature. "He said he would. I asked him to contact Cook, though, by way of the servant's entrance."

Her mother's relief spread about her like a cool fog. "That should pass. Your father doesn't like for us to have visitors."

"I think the colonel understands, Mama, about Father, I

mean."

Mama sighed wistfully. "Good," she said after a moment. "Do you suppose he'll be able to find the person who killed the sergeant?"

Shironne bit her lip as the brush caught a snarl in her curly hair. "I don't know, Mama. Something we looked at is just wrong."

Her two younger sisters came into the bedroom to have their hair brushed, and their conversation came to an end.

* * *

Shironne played with her cup of chocolate in the morning, still unable to place what she'd missed at the sergeant's flat. It seemed to come close, only to slip away like a fish in a pond. The landlady had cleaned everything and told the lieutenant she'd donated his clothes and blankets to the poor, which left the colonel with very little to investigate.

The second housemaid slipped into her room to take her breakfast tray. "Miss," she whispered conspiratorially, "there's someone in the kitchen to see you."

Shironne located her sturdiest slippers, put them on, and then hurried down the back stairs, avoiding the other servants on the way. She halted on the landing though, her mouth hanging open, when the missing idea came swimming within reach.

She found Lieutenant Kassannan waiting for her under Cook's stern eye. "The colonel would like to speak with you again," the lieutenant said when Shironne approached the servants' table. "He has an idea."

"I think I do, as well."

Curiosity surged in the woman's mind, quickly hidden away. "The colonel told me to get your mother's permission first, miss. I left the carriage waiting on the next street over, and I've brought your hat."

Shironne grinned. She *owned* the silly hat now. Her mother came down the servants' stair a moment later, evidently fetched by the second housemaid as well.

"The colonel would like to borrow your daughter again, Madam," the lieutenant told her. "If you're willing."

Shironne sensed her mother's worry. "I'd like to go. I've figured something out, and I need to tell him. I'll be careful, Mama. No one will see me."

"Sweetheart, let the colonel take care of this. You've done what you promised."

"Mama, please, I want to do this. I can be helpful."

"The colonel said we should offer her a job," the lieutenant added.

"Was he serious?" Shironne asked, her own curiosity echoed by her mother's.

"Half-way to, miss. You're young, but he would certainly be willing to take you on when you come of age."

Awfully far away, Shironne thought. "Mama, do you think I could?"

Her mother sighed, her mind turning quickly. "I suppose you must, but I want you to promise me . . ."

In the end, there were about ten things she had to pledge. In addition to not being seen, heard, or injured, she promised to stay with the lieutenant or the colonel at all times. Shironne doubted she could stick to it. She had a talent for falling into trouble.

* * *

"Miss Anjir," the colonel said as she entered his office, "I spoke to our surgeon last night. We may have proceeded under a false assumption."

"We assumed a man killed him."

"Very good," he said.

Shironne pictured in her mind the way the knife must have gone in and come out, angled sharply. She could only think of one way it had happened. "She used both hands to stab him, raised like this, above her head and then coming down, sir."

"And what could you deduce from that?"

"Well, I don't know how tall he was, sir."

The colonel came nearer. "About six inches shorter than me," he said. He held out a hand and raised her gloved fingers to it. "So, the wound would have come about this high off the ground."

She felt his hand, trying to fix the height in her mind. It was too high for her to stab at herself, not with any strength behind it. If she stood on her toes, it might make the difference. "A little taller than me, then?"

"Short of average," the colonel agreed.

"Everyone thinks I'm a little girl because I'm short," Shironne lamented.

"You've disabused us of that notion," the colonel told her. "I was, however, severely castigated by the surgeon for involving you in this."

"You didn't involve me, sir. I involved myself." She drew herself up, trying to look taller. "Well, I didn't catch it yesterday, but I wonder if maybe the woman lives in the boarding house."

"Excuse me?" the colonel said.

"She was barefoot and she walked straight out the door. No one goes out a door and then stops to put their shoes on— it would be remarked. I don't think she ever went outside. She must live in the same building."

"Might it be the landlady?" the lieutenant asked.

"I think she likely sold off his property," the colonel answered, "enough to feel guilty about. She's too tall anyway."

"If I could go to there again, I might be able to find her," Shironne said.

"How?"

"I think I might recognize her if I ran into her."

"We don't have any better lead, sir," the lieutenant said. The colonel reluctantly agreed.

Once they reached the boarding house again, he helped Shironne down from the carriage, silly hat wobbling on her head. They made their way back up to the sergeant's rooms.

Shironne stopped inside the doorway. She knelt, removing one glove to feel the threshold. Dozens of people had crossed through, boots dropping street dust and horse dung in tiny bits all about. Near the edge of the doorway, she found a trace remembrance of the woman's bare, bloodstained foot. She told the colonel.

"Would you recognize her if you touched her?"

"I might, sir." Shironne laid her hand over the print, trying to get a feel for the woman. Her feet had been dirty, with that taste of blood on them, but Shironne separated out her sense of the skin and sweat from all the distractions. She rose awkwardly, the lieutenant's hand coming under her elbow to help her rise. "Maybe I could touch all the doorknobs."

The colonel thought amusement at her. "The landlady will think we're insane. Lieutenant Kassannan, why don't you go inform the woman we're going to search the premises."

The lieutenant hurried away.

"Can you do that, sir?" Shironne asked.

"On your say-so? Certainly. So, how do we proceed?"

"Perhaps if I feel each of the doorknobs, I might know if she touched one."

"Well, then, let's take one floor at a time." He led her down the hallway, grasped her gloved hand and laid it against a doorframe.

She felt for the handle with her other hand and cringed. "Ew. He should wash before he eats."

"I hope you realize the vast majority of people won't wash enough to satisfy your tastes."

Shironne laughed. "I suppose not, sir."

They tried every door on that hallway. She found a great deal of filth, but nothing relevant to the murder.

The landlady returned with the lieutenant in time to witness Shironne's confrontation with the last door. "You don't have any right to do this," she hissed, but scurried away when the colonel corrected that assumption.

"She doesn't want us here," Shironne noted.

"Don't let it concern you." He led her to the next floor, and she proceeded to touch all the doors, finding nothing.

The stairwell to the fourth floor narrowed, forcing the colonel to walk behind her. The pine railing under her bare fingers bore the taste of only a few different hands, oil and dirt and sweat worn into the wood. "She's been here," Shironne told the colonel.

His patience turned to anticipation. Shironne sensed the lieutenant tensing as well. She located the last step and stopped on the landing. "Is the ceiling low?" she asked.

"Yes," the colonel answered.

Shironne suspected he must be stooping, given the pinched sound of his voice. "How far to the door?"

"The first is three feet ahead and two feet to your right."

She followed his directions. The knob felt only of a man. "Not this one, sir."

"Ten feet down the hallway," he said.

She walked ahead, trailing her gloved hand against the wall. She felt at the knob once she'd located the door. "Um, she has touched this one, sir."

"Kassannan, go ahead." The colonel's hand settled on Shironne's shoulder, drawing her back behind him.

The lieutenant passed Shironne in the cramped hallway, and rapped on the door. "Army Investigations. Open up."

Shironne heard no response.

"How certain are you about this?" the colonel asked.

"I know she touched the doorknob. That doesn't mean she lives here, sir."

"We're at the end of a hall. Nowhere else to go."

The lieutenant knocked again.

Shironne heard the sound of feet on the floor inside then. "I heard something, sir."

"So did I," he said. "Let me, Kassannan."

The colonel pulled away from her. Shironne heard something strike the door and realized he must have kicked it. The sound came again. She heard a crash as the door gave, banging into the wall behind it.

"Army," he called as he stepped into the room, away from the hallway. The lieutenant followed, leaving Shironne standing alone there.

Fear prickled through the hallway. Shironne fought it, uncertain whether it was her own. She did fear abandonment in unknown places.

She laid her gloved hand on the wall and felt along it, seeking the door again. Following would be better than being alone. She found the doorframe and stepped into the room. A garret apartment, she decided. The colonel must have had to bend down to get in through the low door.

The room smelled dirty, faint hints of soured milk and urine making her wrinkle her nose. She heard the colonel speaking to the lieutenant, their muffled voices indicating they'd passed into a different room.

Shironne took a step in that direction, but stopped when her foot touched something unexpected on the floor. She tried tapping about and discovered there were objects all about her, small things that would surely trip her should she try to run. Something large huddled on the floor to her left, fabric like a jacket or blanket. Fear welled again, causing her breath to go short.

"Not in the closet, sir," the lieutenant called from far away.

"I found an access to the next apartment. Go back and get the girl."

Shironne stood frozen, very aware of the unidentified things on the floor. Dread beat through her senses. A board creaked behind her, and she heard the whisper of bare feet. A hand tangled into her braid, yanking her close against a wiry body. Her oversized hat tumbled away.

"Sir," the lieutenant called. "She's in here."

The woman held Shironne, trembling limbs pinning her. She wasn't terribly large but she had the strength of desperation.

Her fear roiled through Shironne's senses. Shironne fought to control her mind, counting silently to restore calm. She tried to breathe slowly. Something cool and metallic pressed against her cheek, shaking in the woman's hand.

"Let her go, ma'am," the lieutenant said.

The woman shifted her grip on Shironne's braid, the back

of her hand coming into contact with Shironne's neck.

"Madam," the colonel said in a reasonable tone. "The girl is not your enemy. Let her go."

The woman shook Shironne by her braid. Her dirty hand brushed Shironne's neck again.

Shironne forced herself to touch the woman's mind. Her thoughts were strangely insistent and repetitive, impossibly chaotic and loud. They protested over and over that she didn't know what she'd done wrong.

"Whatever did the sergeant do to you? Why did you kill him?" Shironne asked, hoping to direct the woman's attention where she wanted it to go. Her questions sparked only uncomprehending fear.

The colonel continued to talk soothingly, as if to a child. The woman jerked Shironne farther away. Something small on the floor shifted under Shironne's foot and only the woman's painful grip on her hair kept her standing.

She focused on the circle pressed to her cheek, recognizing it for what it was. She extended her senses through the metal, feeling the touch of the sergeant's hands on it. Metal was always easy.

"The gun . . ." Shironne began.

A shot sounded, deafening in the garret room. Blood, hot and personal, sprayed across Shironne's face. The woman jerked away from her, dragging her down to the floor. Shironne yelped at a sudden flare of pain.

She felt the colonel's hands on her shoulders then, steadying her. He wiped at her face with a piece of starched linen, smoothing away most of the blood splattered across her cheek. She could feel his worry crowding around her. "I'm so sorry, Miss Anjir," he said. "I didn't realize she had a way to get back around behind us."

Shironne calmed her breathing, easier now the woman's beating panic had faded. "She's insane, Colonel."

"Was," the lieutenant said flatly. "She's dead."

"Damn," the colonel said.

Shironne took a deep breath. The colonel gave her the handkerchief and she began to scrub at her hand with it. "Um, the gun wasn't loaded."

Clicking metallic sounds followed. "She's right, sir," the lieutenant said.

"Well, the fact that she's in possession of it indicates she had some involvement in the sergeant's death." The colonel sighed, irritation surrounding him. "What a mess. Now we'll never know what happened."

"Sir, I had to take the shot," the lieutenant said.

"You're not at fault, Kassannan. I should never have brought Miss Anjir up here in the first place."

Shironne sensed his frustration. "Sir, I could find out what . . . I mean, why . . . if we don't wait too long."

His mind turned, weighing consequences and curiosity. "Are you willing to try?"

She nodded, suddenly aware that her scalp hurt. She touched her gloved hand to the sore spot.

"I'm afraid she ripped out a bit of your hair."

The realization brought tears to her eyes, the pain sharpening. Her mother would be upset and would never let her work for the colonel again. "Is it bad enough my mother will notice?" she asked, blinking away the tears.

"I will tell her myself," the colonel said sternly.

Pain washed through the room, sobbing accompanying it. "You killed her," a voice cried— the landlady.

"Sit down on the floor, ma'am," the lieutenant ordered. "We have questions for you."

"You killed her," the woman repeated.

"Yes," the lieutenant said. "Now sit down before I do the

same to you. You've abetted a crime."

The landlady's pain turned to anguish. She began sobbing noisily. "I tried. I tried. I tried so hard."

"Come with me," the colonel said to Shironne, ignoring the woman. He replaced Shironne's hat, helped her stand, and walked her carefully through the room.

"What's all over the floor?" she asked.

"Toys and wooden blocks. A baby blanket, I think."

Shironne could smell the blood, strong and metallic, almost tasting it with her too-sensitive tongue. She reached out with her foot and contacted the body. Kneeling next to the dead woman, she felt for the woman's face with her bare hand. The colonel put his hand on her sleeve and directed her away from the ruined part of the woman's face.

"Don't touch her!" the landlady cried.

The colonel's anger flared, but he said nothing, compassion replacing it.

"Quiet," the lieutenant said to the landlady.

Shironne pressed her hand to the dead woman's skin. Warm and soft still, the blood no longer moved under the surface. Everything had halted, stopped in its path.

She reached deeper, searching for the scattered leaves of

memory in the woman's mind. They'd had no time to decay yet, each preserved clearly for her to see. Shironne touched one and then another, confirming what she'd suspected when the woman had still been alive. She wasn't sane. She'd lost her child and then her mind.

Shironne found a distinct memory of Sergeant Merha speaking with the woman in the foyer of the boarding house. He'd been polite and kind. That simple act alone triggered her obsession with him. He was meant to give her another child, she'd believed, only he hadn't wanted her. She waited in his bed, but he didn't want to lie with her. In her desperation, she struck him.

"I don't think she realized what she'd done, sir," Shironne said, drawing away. "She knew she'd done something wrong, because her sister ordered her up here and wouldn't let her come down again, but I don't think she understood she killed him. Yesterday when you ran into her downstairs, she was waiting by his door for him to come back."

"I won't send her to a madhouse," the landlady sobbed. "I'll keep her safe. I promised."

They found the sergeant's army-issued knife in the landlady's kitchen. Even under the film of soap, Shironne could still feel his blood on the blade. Together with the gun, the colonel claimed, they had evidence enough, and the landlady confessed it all.

* * *

Her mother was furious— quietly, tearfully so, but furious.

The colonel had taken her back to the Army Square where she'd been able to clean her hands and face to her own satisfaction. Lieutenant Kassannan sponged the stains from her worn red tunic, and Shironne re-braided her hair, hoping the sticky and painful patch would heal quickly. The colonel was correct in believing she'd not be able to hide it.

Sitting at the servants' table in their kitchen, he confessed everything. "Madam, I wouldn't lie to you," he finished.

"Because you know very well I would sense it if you did," her mother said in a trembling voice. Her hand stroked Shironne's hair, easing over the painful spot. "I shouldn't have agreed to this."

"Madam, I could sorely use someone with her talents. I would like her to work for me from time to time, if . . ."

"Colonel, I let her have her way this time because she gave

her word. Not again."

"Madam," the colonel said in a serious tone. "Your child has a very rare talent. Is it not her duty to use it for the good of others?"

Shironne wondered how he knew what effect that word would have on her mother. Most people with gifts were expected to enter the priesthood, but that fate had never appealed to her. Working for the colonel might prove an excellent alternative. "Mama, I think I could be really good at this."

"I will," her mother said after a moment, "consider it."

"That, Madam Anjir," the colonel said softly, "is enough for today." Shironne heard the rattle of paper. "I would like for you to memorize this. It's my address."

Her mother radiated a strange mixture of guilt and hope. "I can't . . ."

"Any hour of the day or night, Madam, you or your daughters may go there. Should you need a safe haven, I mean. My servants will know your names." He'd made sure Shironne memorized it in the carriage on the way back to the house. "After all, I did warn you that I'm one of the prince's closest friends. That makes me almost family, Madam."

Shironne heard him rise and move toward the servant's

door.

"You shouldn't interfere, Colonel," her mother said without any heat behind her words. "In any way."

"Hmm. I'm just . . . the interfering sort, I suppose," he said, and then was gone.

THE END

Endings

This story takes place takes place about six months before the beginning of *Dreaming Death*. Once again, we have Shironne embroiled in the search for a criminal, but this time, in the end, the crime points closer to home than she and Colonel Cerradine like.

Although I intended this story for the same magazine that published the previous story, it was not to be as that magazine's next year was its last. However, I wanted to include it here because it covers an event mentioned in *Dreaming Death*.

Endings

If there was anything that Jon Cerradine hated, it was not being able to fix things.

Jaw clenched, he stared down at the blanket-wrapped body in the wagon. It seemed cruel for a soldier to die in such a senseless accident. And personal, because the woman whose body lay carefully swaddled in that wagon had been one of *his* handpicked people. *Cerradine's children*, as the general liked to call them.

Now he would have to tell her husband, one of his closest friends. Now the workers in his office would all grieve together. Many lived in the same building she and her husband had. Her death was personal for all of them.

The sun was slow to rise this early in the spring, but it now illuminated the scene of the accident that had taken her life. Soot marks coated the alleyway, and an acrid stench clung in the air, dryness irritating Cerradine's eyes. The nearer wall of a cotton mill's granite façade had blown outward when a gas line exploded. One side wall still bowed outward dangerously, hastily constructed supports shoring it up. The alleyway was almost impassable. A pair of police officers stood inside the building's remains questioning the mill's owner, a barrel-chested man in a heavily-embroidered tunic with an ashen look to his brown skin.

Lieutenant Aldassa strode toward the wagon, his boots crunching on bits of broken stone. He looked grim. "Owner got lucky," he said, his head tilting back that man's direction. "Gas valve inside the mill was shut off. Would have blown down the entire building otherwise. Fire never even caught. Ready to go back, Colonel?

Cerradine nodded and began picking his way back to his carriage. Lieutenant Hanna Kassannan had simply been in the wrong place last night.

* * *

It didn't seem fair to Shironne that she had to share other people's dreams, particularly the distressing ones. She trudged up the steps of the Army's administration building. Her slippers dragged on the stone steps, the sound betraying her weariness. She'd barely slept at all, troubled by her dream. She clutched at the crystal focus in her tunic pocket, sensing its clean lines even through several layers of fabric. Concentrating on its orderly lines helped her clear away the tatters of the dream that still clouded her waking mind.

These dreams had gone on for years now, some more urgent that others. This one seemed almost personal to her, compelling her to report in even though this wasn't one of her usual days to be here. The colonel's workers loved schedules, but there were times when schedules should be ignored.

Her mother leaned nearer and slid a hand under Shironne's elbow, her bracelet tinkling and the scent of vanilla and sandalwood drifting with her. "Stop now," she said in her soft voice. "The door is right in front of you."

She should have known that, but concentrating on the focus had kept her from counting steps. Shironne raised one gloved hand to feel for the latch, opened the door, stepped inside, and turned right. People passed in the hallway, minds busy. Shironne walked along the hallway, her fingers brushing the wall as she counted the doorways. She didn't need her mother's prompt to recognize the one she sought.

The army's *Office for Intelligence and Investigation* bustled, not with its usual efficient air, but with an angry, aching kind of busyness, as if they'd all stubbed their toes and danced to mute the throbbing. The air of pain tore at Shironne's overwrought senses. She clenched her jaw to force down sudden tears. *The hurt isn't mine,* she reminded herself, gripping the crystal again.

"Madam Anjir?"

Shironne recognized Lieutenant Aldassa, the colonel's aide. Aldassa wasn't ignoring her, as many people did when they realized she was blind. He was simply trying to set her mother at ease.

"We'd like to speak to Colonel Cerradine, if that's possible," her mother began.

The colonel *always* made time to speak with her mother. It was more than mere courtesy on the colonel's part. Over the last few years, he'd developed a strong interest in her mother's well-being, although he'd never done or said anything overly familiar. Yet somehow, he'd convinced Shironne's father to move out of the family house a couple of years ago. Shironne certainly appreciated her father's absence. Her mother did, too, even if she never said so aloud.

"If the two of you would follow me," Aldassa replied, "I'll notify the colonel that you're here."

There was a small waiting area in the back of the office where soldiers or visitors passing through wouldn't see them.

They always took her mother there to prevent her presence in the office from being noted. Mama worried that people would talk and, as a politician's wife, she naturally garnered attention. She abhorred the idea of scandal.

Mama led her down the short hallway in the lieutenant's wake. Once they'd reached their destination, she placed Shironne's hand on the back of a wooden chair. Shironne flipped her braid out of the way and settled on the hard seat. She heard her mother sitting a second later, the tinkling of her bracelet's bells accompanied by the faint rustle of silk as she adjusted her layers of petticoats and tunic, likely gracefully. Her mother did everything gracefully.

Shironne tugged her scarf away from her face. She suspected her mother went veiled as well, although she hadn't asked.

"May I ask what this is about, Madam?" Aldassa was all efficient attention now, his distress pushed to the back of his mind. "Miss Anjir wasn't scheduled to come in today."

Shironne answered instead. "Um, I had a dream last night, Lieutenant."

She sensed Aldassa's emotional retreat, the warmth of his attention ebbing from her senses like a blanket pulling away.

"One of *those* dreams?" he asked in a guarded tone.

"Yes," she said, "someone died."

For a second his thoughts spun, barely tangible at the edge of her awareness. "I'll let the colonel know immediately," was all he said before he took himself away.

Shironne had worked with Aldassa long enough to know that he wanted evidence, not suppositions. No matter how agitated he was, he wouldn't jump to conclusions about the dream or its meaning.

A moment later, Colonel Cerradine himself came to fetch them, easily identifiable by the smell of his cologne and his long stride. "Madam Anjir, Miss Anjir. Would you come with me back to my office?"

Her mother rose and didn't answer his query for a second, likely gathering her thoughts. The colonel pushed reassurance at them as if mentally repeating that they were *safe*. He was skilled at that, holding his emotions out so they could sense them.

"Colonel," her mother began, "I don't think I should be gone from home too long. I wondered if...if I might leave her with you?"

Irritation suddenly flared around him.

"I have many things I need to do today," her mother added.

Shironne suspected her mother's hands were held tight together, a beseeching pose. If she stayed away from the house too long, Father would hear about it. He might come around then, demanding to know where his wife had been. Even though he no longer lived with them, he still controlled the family's tight purse strings and could make their lives more uncomfortable.

"I understand, Madam Anjir," the colonel said in a cool tone.

And he *did* understand. Shironne knew the colonel didn't approve. Not of her father. Not of how he treated Mama.

"If you could send her home later," Mama said, "then I can hire a cab..."

"My driver will take you home, Madam Anjir," the colonel said firmly. They had this discussion *every* time her mother accompanied her. "If you'll wait here, Miss Anjir," the colonel added, speaking to Shironne now, "I'll escort your mother out to the carriage pool and come right back."

"Yes, sir."

The colonel moved away with her mother, down the hallway and beyond the range where Shironne could easily pick up his feelings. She occupied herself instead by puzzling at the emotions running like a common thread through the office. Had her fears been correct?

Before she could settle on an answer, the colonel returned, his mind plotting and locked away from her. "What about your dream, Miss Anjir?"

"It was one of *those* dreams." *Everyone* in this office knew what she meant by that.

There was a man up at the palace who dreamed his way into others' deaths. He was their private guardian in those last moments, their Angel of Death. Since Shironne's ability to sense emotions was far stronger than others', she also shared his dreams. On and off since she was eleven, she would fall into a dream about someone's death, always a bad end. But she came out of the dreams with memories that helped her—and the colonel's people—find the killers. That was worth putting up with all the vagaries of her gift. She could get justice for the victims.

The colonel's attention sharpened. "Tell me about it."

She took a deep breath, forcing away the surge of tension that had accompanied this dream, and started from the beginning. "I was following someone. Hunting them. Then I was waiting, watching. Someone came up behind me and I turned to...confront them. I remember hearing a loud sound...a gunshot. And then another. I remember falling to my knees. I was shot, sir, but then I woke up."

The recitation troubled him. "Do you know who you were? In the dream?"

She touched her focus in her pocket, and quickly moved her hand away. The colonel had said before that she could do without it, that it was a crutch. "No, sir...but I do think I was wearing trousers."

"Trousers?"

"Not like mine," she clarified. Most women wore trousers under their petticoats to stave off the cold. Hers were loose save around the ankles, while the ones in the dream had fit...well, like the trousers she'd seen soldiers wearing before she'd lost her sight. "I walked differently. And I had different boots on...um, polished boots, not slippers. I saw a streetlight reflect off them."

In those dreams, she could *see*, a regular reminder of what she'd lost.

"Were you a man or a woman?"

"A woman, I think," she said. "And the only women I know who wear trousers like that are your people here, sir." The furious mood in these halls today made her suspect she'd guessed correctly.

The colonel sighed and she heard him rise. He came closer, until she could smell the wool of his uniform, the faint tang of gun oil, and the hint of cologne. "I'm going to ask you to do something very difficult. We have a body in our morgue. I'd like you to go over to the hospital with me, because I'd like to know the truth of what happened to her."

Cold spread through her body. If the body was here, in the army's morgue, then it *had* to be one of the colonel's workers. She'd been right, when she had very much wanted not to be.

"Lieutenant Kassannan?" she whispered.

* * *

If Shironne was correct, they'd been lied to.

One thing Cerradine knew for certain, every time—every single time—Mikael Lee dreamed his way into someone's death, it was murder. The young man, an aide to the prince who worked up at the palace, had been inflicting his dreams on Shironne for years now. Sometimes he would come out and help them track down a killer, but usually when it involved army personnel, Shironne was the one who felt compelled to help, no matter how hard on her it was.

Her brown eyes glittered with tears now, her expressive face displaying the emotion he'd been trained not to show. She twisted her gold silk scarf in her lap, wrinkling it. "I'm so sorry. How is the captain?"

That was the worst part—his attached medical examiner, Captain Aron Kassannan, had lost his wife last night. Cerradine suspected Aron was still in shock over the news. "Hard to tell. But if we can find the truth, that will help."

Shironne had worked with both of the Kassannans. Hanna had saved her life once when a madwoman had taken Shironne hostage, and later had taken it on herself to teach Shironne several ways to defend herself should she be caught in a similar situation again. Aron Kassannan had instructed Shironne in both anatomy and chemistry, helping her to shape her abilities into a tool for finding murderers. She didn't know Hanna as well as the rest of his workers had, but that didn't mean Hanna's death wouldn't pain her.

Once Shironne gathered herself, he escorted her across the green from the administrative offices to the military hospital where the morgue lay tucked away in the basement. He drew her down the back stairs and opened the door to the morgue. It smelled unpleasant, the scents of stale blood and decay never quite eradicated by the carbolic acid used to clean the place.

When the door shut behind them, the surgeon turned to survey them. Cerradine wasn't truly surprised at who stood there, even though he'd ordered Kassannan to go home.

Shironne clapped a gloved hand over her mouth, her eyes welling with tears again. She must be reflecting Kassannan's anguish. Cerradine put a hand on her shoulder to reassure her, wishing calmness at her as she grasped at that crystal she kept in her pocket.

"Aron," he told the surgeon, "you can't be objective about this."

"This is just a body now. Hanna's gone," Kassannan said softly.

Cerradine had to clamp down his own worry at that flat response. *No, Aron isn't doing well.*

Nearly as tall as he was but with a heavier build, Aron Kassannan could pass for Cerradine's younger brother. They had similar features and coloring, save for the hair. Kassannan's was still dark, while Cerradine's prematurely white hair had come from his late father. And Aron's face was lined with exhaustion this morning. He'd been up most of the night. He turned halfway to face Cerradine and caught sight Shironne for the first time. "What is Miss Anjir doing here?"

"I want her to look at Hanna's body."

Kassannan stared at him dully for a moment. "Why?"

"She might be able to tell us exactly how or why Hanna died."

"*Hel's tits*, a building fell on her," Kassannan snapped, tossing the blood-stained towel he held into a basin set on the floor. "That's it, Jon."

Shironne cringed at his angry outburst and then shook her head as if trying to dash the emotion away. It was one of the most important rules a sensitive ever learned; protect yourself from others' emotions.

Kassannan frowned and rubbed at his temples. "I apologize, Miss Anjir."

He'd worked with Miss Anjir almost from the beginning. He knew what bothered her and what didn't, likely better than anyone else among the office's personnel, even Cerradine himself. *Surely, Aron realizes why she's here.*

"Just let us do this, Aron," Cerradine said. "Please."

Kassannan's eyes moved between him and Shironne, and Cerradine could see comprehension flare in his eyes. Jaw clenched, Kassannan strode to the door and threw himself onto the wooden chair that waited there. He dropped his head into his hands.

Cerradine set one hand under Shironne's elbow. "Sure about this?" he whispered.

She nodded, and he led her forward to the table. He drew back the sheet that covered Hanna's face. Kassannan had been cleaning his wife's body, the broken features washed free of blood. Cerradine still cringed at the sight.

"Um, does she look bad?" Shironne asked in a small voice.

Shironne must have picked up *his* reaction to the sight. Cerradine pitched his voice so that Kassannan wouldn't overhear. "Yes."

"Oh," she said ruefully, eyes glittering again. Her gloved hand touched the pocket that held her focus again, a sign she was struggling to calm herself.

For her sake, Cerradine quietly explained where and how the body was found. The sheet still covered Hanna's body, but her face gave some clue as to the violence of the explosion. The blast had sent stones flying in all directions with enough force behind them to break bones and tear away skin. Battered flesh stretched across a shattered visage. A jagged edge of bone protruded above the hollow of her left cheek.

Undeterred, Shironne frowned, stripped off her gloves, and tucked them into a pocket on the seam of her blue tunic. She drew a careful breath and extended her arm.

Usually Kassannan was the one to direct her during her visits to the morgue, but Cerradine had done this once or twice when the captain wasn't available. He grasped her sleeve to lift her arm. "Where?"

"Her face?" Her voice trembled a bit.

"Bad," he warned.

Shironne drew a shuddering breath and squared her narrow shoulders. "Go ahead."

He placed her naked hand on the unbroken side of Hanna's face, but Shironne lifted her fingers immediately. "Enough?" he asked.

After taking a deep breath, the girl shook her head. "No, sir. I can do this. I *need* to."

Cerradine stepped back. He understood that need. It was why most of his staff had risen in the early hours to investigate a death. It was why Aron Kassannan was here, ever though he'd been ordered to go home.

Shironne laid her hand against the side of Hanna's face again and stood there a moment, her lower lip caught between her teeth. When she lifted her hand, Cerradine moved closer. Her head turned in his direction. "She is the person I dreamed about, sir. No doubt of that."

That meant Hanna had been murdered. "How can you tell?"

"All the events in her head line up with the dream, sir. Her memories are all disordered and broken, though. Maybe because the skull is damaged. I don't know. I can only find little bits, and what I'm finding doesn't have any relevance. I...I don't think it was a quick death." She whispered that last bit.

She didn't *know?* Mikael Lee usually dreamed for hours when this happened, from the moment where the threat occurred until the death. They were not *normal* dreams. "Did you not dream the death? The whole thing?"

"I made myself wake up," she said. "It was too...wrong."

Is she strong enough now to resist her Angel of Death's ability to drag her into his dreams? That would be worth a discussion with Mikael's sponsors up at the palace. Usually no one escaped his broadcasted dreams. The fact that Shironne had managed to do so was interesting. He tucked that mental query away for later.

He glanced back at the door instead, hoping the captain hadn't overheard. "Why do you say it wasn't quick?"

"The memories I can find," Shironne said quietly, "the ones that were the last, were all about her husband and things she wanted to remember. She knew she was dying." She turned back to the table and asked, "Can you put my hand on her shoulder?"

He grasped Shironne's sleeve, using it to lift her hand again. Standing on her toes, she reached across to the other side of the sheet-covered body, placing one hand on each shoulder. He knew the sheet only *muted* the impressions her over-sensitive skin picked up. "What are you doing now?"

After a long moment, she answered. "There's lead. It's flattened out, tangled in the vertebrae." She lifted her hands and laid them farther down on the body but closer together, narrowing the window between her fingers. "Definitely a bullet, sir."

"Bullet?" Kassannan asked, his mouth closing in a tight line. While Cerradine's attention had fixed on Shironne, Kassannan had slipped closer.

"Shironne, step back," Cerradine directed. She moved away a few steps, holding her hands out from her clothing. She would need to wash her hands now; she hated it when she had foreign matter on her skin.

Kassannan paused for a second, looking down at his wife's

broken face, and then carefully tucked the sheet around her body. He turned the stiffening form, exposing a mottled and torn back.

Cerradine made himself think of this as a corpse—not his trusted lieutenant. In places, her discolored skin gave way to exposed muscle.

"There's so much damage I would never have thought to look for it," Kassannan said in a strained voice. "Where did you say it was?"

Shironne spoke from behind them. "Between the fifth and sixth thoracic vertebrae, Captain."

"Why don't you sit down," Cerradine suggested to her. "There's a chair by the door, about twelve steps directly behind you."

She tapped her way back toward the door, located the chair and sat, her hands still held away from her clothes.

Kassannan ran cautious fingers along the ruined curve of his wife's back. "I think this is it," Kassannan said, and then spun out a stream of curses. "There is a bullet in there. I can see it now."

Kassannan crossed to where drawers on the wall hid his surgical implements, but Cerradine intercepted him. "Aron, this changes things. It's a murder investigation now. I want you to hand this over to Farhana."

For a second, Kassannan didn't answer. "I can't do that, sir."

"It's an order." Cerradine met Kassannan's eyes. "Get out of here. Send me Farhana, and get one of the orderlies to fetch Aldassa for me. Go home."

Kassannan nodded, jerked off his work-apron, and headed toward the door of the morgue. He stopped near Shironne, though. "Who did this?"

Shironne turned her face halfway toward his. "I don't know, sir. Not yet. But I'll find out."

* * *

Shironne clung to a hand strap in the carriage, trying to decide what vital piece she was missing. The colonel had gone to notify the proper authorities that his officer had been murdered. Since they had first marked it as an accident, the police had to be told that it was clearly not. That would be an awkward and delicate conversation. The colonel wouldn't delegate that task to anyone else.

Not that the colonel is particularly diplomatic. But he wanted to see the police commissioner's face when he asked his questions, he'd claimed, so he'd left Shironne in Aldassa's charge. Fortunately, Aldassa was thoroughly familiar with her peculiar methods of investigation.

In turn, she was familiar with Aldassa's orderly doggedness. Now that he knew Lieutenant Kassannan's death wasn't an accident, Aldassa would stay on the killer's trail until there was justice. She wanted to help him do so, and so she agreed to go view the scene with him.

One Ensign Navinne had joined them in one of the army's carriages. The young woman sat on the other side next to Aldassa. She'd sounded pleased to be given a task that would get her out from behind a desk but, like Aldassa, Navinne kept her mind carefully neutral. She said little as the carriage began to move.

Shironne had no idea what sort of duties Hanna Kassannan usually had beyond teaching visiting Larossan girls to defend themselves. "What was Lieutenant Kassannan doing last night?" she asked Aldassa. "When she died, I mean."

"Hmmm. Not sure," Aldassa said. "Supposed to have been with a partner, watching for a dealer near the Lower Town

Bridge. Jonnada—the partner—reports in 'bout two hours later, saying she slipped off."

The calm tone of his voice didn't match the anger she felt seeping out of him. "You don't believe that."

"Can't say I do. Not like her to slip off."

"Do you think he's the one who shot her?"

Navinne said nothing, but Shironne sensed mild distaste from the young woman, similar to her own reaction to leeks. This Ensign Jonnada must have gotten onto her bad side.

"Don't like to think that, either," Aldassa finally answered. "But possible."

"A dealer in what?" Shironne asked, trying to work out how that fit in with her dream. Aldassa's amusement peeked out from behind his irritation. Inside, he was laughing at her question. "Am I supposed to know?" she asked him.

"Drugs, Miss Anjir. Illegal ones," he said. "Opium, blue sky, hashish. That sort of dealer."

"Oh, I see," she said, trying to sound worldly. At least she'd managed to lighten his mood, even if it had come at her expense. "So, who might have killed Lieutenant Kassannan?"

"Don't know," Aldassa said. "Always suspect the husband first..."

She couldn't imagine anyone believing that. "Captain Kassannan?"

"Usually we would talk to him first," Aldassa said, "but he has an alibi."

"Of course he does," she returned. "No one could seriously think he did it."

"I could, Miss Anjir," Aldassa said with complete sincerity. "I don't let my emotions make that kind of decision for me. In this case, though, I know it's not possible. He was at my flat, talking my ear off last night."

"Captain Kassannan was at your flat?"

"We live in the same building," Aldassa told her. "He had a fight with Hanna, came to brood over it, like always."

Shironne pressed her lips together. "Did they fight a lot?"

"Yes," Navinne answered in a laughing tone.

"Hmm. Just how they talked, Miss Anjir," Aldassa added. "Liana and I never had a fight yet. She's quiet, not like Hanna."

Shironne had met Aldassa's wife, Liana, a young seamstress of Larossan descent—*not* military. She could see why they never fought; they probably never even spoke in that household. That might be better than a house where people fought. She'd heard enough of that from her own parents.

The carriage groaned to a stop, saving her from admitting that. "Where are we?"

Aldassa moved past her to open the carriage door and stepped down. "Larossan New Quarter, near the rubber factory."

She could smell that. The air felt dirty against her face, steam and smoke from the factories bearing all manner of nasty things she didn't want touching her overly-sensitive skin. She wrapped her scarf over her face, hoping the thin layer of silk would mute the feel of the wind's dirty fingers touching her.

Once he'd helped her down from the carriage, Aldassa lifted one of her gloved hands and laid it on his arm. "This way."

The footing was uneven and, as such, treacherous. At one point, Shironne stumbled on a loose piece of something. Aldassa helped get her back on her feet and then stood motionless as Navinne moved somewhere a few feet away. Reaching a hand into her pocket, Shironne wrapped her fingers around her focus to help clear her mind. She swallowed her nervousness at being in this unknown place. Aldassa *would* keep her safe. "What are we doing?"

He took a moment to reply. "Trying to look at this place with new eyes."

"New eyes?" It would be handy if *she* could do that.

Aldassa sighed. "Change my preconceptions. I came here early this morning, but thought this was an accident. Now I'm trying to see this scene as if someone did it intentionally."

He meant the explosion, she decided. "To hide shooting her?"

"Hmm."

The humming sound meant he wanted her to stop talking. Aldassa didn't radiate irritation as her father would have, but his mind spiraled in tight coils of thought. She would only be distracting him.

He made a clucking sound then. "Stupid. Not much blood."

He meant there wasn't enough blood where Kassannan's body had been found. She'd been killed elsewhere. "What does it look like?"

"Lots of broken stone, sprayed out like a fan. Most of it here, but little bits spreading a long way away. Shifted out of the way where they dug Kassannan out."

That explained the bad footing. The gritty-dusty feel of the wind touching her cheeks told of smoke—gas-smoke, not wood, hot against the air. "Did anything else burn?"

"No. Only the gas sitting in the pipes. Immediate explosion blew down the façade, but main gas valve to the building was shut off. Thought it was fortuitous, not intentional. Should have suspected it."

He'd been looking at it with the wrong eyes. "You mean they came in, opened the gas main and let some gas build up, shut off the gas main, and then blew up the...whatever they blew up?"

"Precisely." His hand touched hers. "You wait here."

Shironne nodded, hoping he wouldn't leave her for long. She heard him moving, the dry sound of stone shifting against stone, dry mortar crunching under his feet.

At the end of the alleyway, she could hear two men talking. Even from that distance, she could sense their avid interest in the soldiers' actions. "Soldier," one of the men called, "what are you doing here? I gave the police my statement already."

"We're expanding the investigation," Aldassa called back.

Shironne heard the crunching sound of one of the men approaching. The other left; she couldn't sense him any longer. The first man passed close to her, worry buzzing about him like flies. An odd scent followed him, one with sickly sweet and musky notes, barely detectable under the smell of hot rubber that clogged the alleyway. It wasn't one of the chemicals Captain Kassannan had taught her to recognize.

"Investigation? I want to get a crew in to start cleaning up," the man protested. "I'll need you to clear out."

"Pallav, isn't it?" Aldassa continued in his most brusque tone, annoyance flaring about him. "We're investigating the murder of an army officer. We'll leave once we're done."

Pallav's worry increased at those words. "Every hour this mill is closed, dozens of people lose their pay, soldier," he argued. "I need to get this cleared out and some sort of a wall back up."

"We'll leave as soon as we're done, sir," Aldassa repeated.

The man stomped off, mumbling under his breath. His apparent anger seemed at odds with the edge of fear Shironne felt from him. She heard Aldassa crunching back in her direction and then caught the faint scent of his perspiration and warm wool.

"Talked to him this morning," Aldassa said. "Let the police take his statement. Stupid. Just not enough blood. If she'd been killed by the blast, with that much damage, I'd expect she'd bleed out. Didn't happen, though. Should have caught that." Shironne decided that Aldassa must be talking to Navinne, but then he added words meant for her. "Let's see, something they would have touched..."

"The gas valve," Navinne said from a few feet away. "That had to have been turned off by someone involved."

Shironne felt better knowing where all three of them stood.

"Well, the owner claimed he didn't do it," Aldassa said. "Said one of the shift managers must have. Let's give it a try."

Aldassa set Shironne's hand on his arm again, and they slowly made their way around the side of the building, Navinne evidently ahead of them. The main valve to this part of the building was at the base of the inner wall destroyed by the blast, he explained. The air about them smelled odd, making the back of Shironne's throat ache. "Are things burned in here?"

"Hardly touched. Lots of rubble on the floor, miss. They've cleared some of the parts of this wall that blew down, but not all of it," Navinne observed. "So...someone let the gas build up in this room and then tossed in a match. The metal frame behind *this* stone wall would have deflected the explosion outward, taking out the outer wall, but leaving most of this one. Gas would have burned out before the beams had a chance to catch. How fortunate for the owner."

Shironne couldn't quite picture what Navinne was describing, but she caught the suspicion under the woman's words. Those who did it would have had to know how the building was laid out.

"Too fortunate," Aldassa said then. "If *I* were hiding a murder, I wouldn't care if I burned down a few buildings. Unless I owned one of them."

An interesting insight into how Aldassa's mind worked, Shironne decided. "Could the owner be involved?"

"Hmm. Why damage his own factory?" He drew her away from the dry room and laid her gloved hand against something metal—a pipe. "Gas valve is here."

Shironne felt along the metal pipe that lead to something far larger that smelled of old, dirty oil and over-warm rubber. "What is this attached to?"

"Engine—gas driven," Aldassa said, a hint of uncertainty. "Big belt that goes up to the ceiling and drives...a bunch of gears...somewhere. No idea what it has to do with cotton."

"Is this a fabric mill?" Now that she thought about it, she could smell fabric. The odor of the rubber factory overlaid everything, but she could just barely taste the burned fibers in the air.

"Yes," Navinne said, the first time she'd spoken in a while. "It's a loom, sir. I worked in a mill while I was trying to get on with the army."

Shironne could sense Aldassa's slow surprise. She heard footsteps as if he was turning in a circle, and he didn't speak for a moment.

"Um, where is the valve again?" Shironne asked.

"Sorry," he said, drawn back to her task. "It's on the bottom of a pipe on the tank, near the ground."

Shironne crouched down, using the side of the tank as a guide. At the base, she located a pipe, and on that, a small lever. "Is this it?"

"Yes."

She stripped off one glove and carefully felt the lever. Many hands had touched it, oil and tiny bits of skin left behind, as well as a great deal of dirt. And then... "I feel blood."

"Hers?" Aldassa asked.

She considered the blood, comparing it mentally with the body she'd touched earlier. "Um, no. A man. Not very old, I think. The blood, I mean, not the man. Maybe as recent as last night."

"How do you know it's a man's blood?" Navinne asked. Aldassa had seen this before, so he didn't question her verdict, but Navinne hadn't worked with her before.

"Um, I can't explain," Shironne admitted. She simply didn't

have words that described what she felt. A man's blood was subtly different from a woman's. "There's something about the blood that says *man* to me."

Navinne made a soft *hmm*, her thoughts carefully neutral.

"You said that in your dream, Kassannan fired her weapon?" Aldassa asked.

"Yes." Shironne concentrated, trying to recall that moment of the dream. "I'm certain of it."

Aldassa's thoughts spun down, all quick calculation. "Kassannan never missed."

* * *

When Cerradine entered his office, Shironne sat in her usual chair. He felt inordinately relieved to see the girl in one piece. She had a talent for landing in trouble.

"I'll go check on that paperwork," Navinne said to Aldassa as she edged out the door.

Cerradine nodded to Aldassa and then turned back to Shironne "Are you all right?"

"Yes, sir." She sat up straighter. "We were just...discussing."

"Discussing?" he prompted when she didn't finish the

thought.

"The explosion had to be set up by someone familiar with the layout of the factory, sir," Aldassa answered instead. "Likely someone aware that there was a danger it could happen."

"Someone who worked there," Cerradine said.

"Or the owner," Aldassa supplied.

"We'll start with him, then." Cerradine trusted Aldassa's instincts about people. "Anything else?"

"Miss Anjir found blood on the gas valve that had been shut off, not Hanna's, she says, so someone else was bleeding at the scene."

He was familiar with statements like that from Shironne. "Any idea whose?"

Shironne shifted. "I don't know, sir, but it came from a man."

He believed her, but her word could never be admitted in court. They would have to find better evidence. "You said that in your dream, Hanna fired her weapon?"

"Yes." Shironne's brow furrowed. "I'm certain of it."

"And Hanna never missed," Aldassa said.

It was something of an adage in the office. Hanna had been a marksman, one of the best. "So, we're positive that a man was involved, and at some point she probably shot him."

"Yes, sir," Aldassa said. "Also, Hanna herself was shot at a point farther down the alley and then moved to where the explosion took place. We found blood there that Miss Anjir verifies is hers."

After examining Hanna's body, Farhana opined that the gunshot hadn't killed her, although it was likely she'd hit her head falling. That she might have been in shock by the time she was moved. Cerradine could only hope the blast quickly ended her pain.

Aldassa shook his head. "She was shot about two buildings down. We thought it was an accident, sir. I don't think any of us went down that far this morning."

"How did you find it this time, then?"

Aldassa laughed shortly. "Geometry. Miss Anjir remembered there was a streetlight in her dream. She told me the angle of the light relative to her shoes in the dream. I figured it out from there, sir."

"Hmm." Cerradine raised his eyebrows. Simple geometry. Aldassa's grasp of detail always impressed him. "So, we definitely have an attempt to hide a murder."

"Absolutely, sir."

Ensign Navinne reappeared in the doorway, a folder in her

hands. "Sir."

Cerradine glanced over at the young woman. One of his more recent recruits, Navinne was eager to prove herself here. Thus far she'd been quite efficient and impressed the lieutenants with her work. "What is it, Ensign?"

"No word on finding Lieutenant Jonnada, sir," she began. "He didn't report for duty this afternoon, but that wasn't a surprise. I wanted to point this out, though." She held out the folder to him. "If you look at the paperwork from the police, you'll see that the same officer who filled out the mill owner's statement around ten this morning is the one who first arrived on the scene late last night—about midnight, he said. That's a very long duty shift."

"Good job catching that." Cerradine told her. It was possible for an officer to be on duty that long, but it was...unusual. "What are the chances of that being a coincidence?"

"Can't give you odds on that, sir," Navinne said with a shrug, handing over the folder.

Cerradine glanced at the two reports. "We need to concentrate on finding Lieutenant Jonnada, then, and this Officer...." He peered at the scribbled signatures. "Ranjan, I think?"

Aldassa suggested sending someone out to check at the City Hospital to see if anyone had gone there with a gunshot wound. "Hanna's gun must still be buried in the rubble," he added. "I'll get a squad of men to start shifting it, sir. The mill's owner is antsy to start cleaning up."

"He can wait." Cerradine looked over at Shironne, who seemed worn down. She'd sat silent through most of that discussion, a rarity for her. Recalling that her mother preferred that Shironne keep as normal a schedule as possible, he added, "Miss Anjir, you've been of tremendous help, but I don't think we have anything else for you to do today. I'll have Ensign Navinne escort you home. That should get you home in time for dinner."

Shironne sighed. "Yes, sir. Will you send for me if you need anything else?"

"Yes, Miss Anjir, and please apologize to your mother for me for keeping you so long. Navinne, would you walk her down to the drivers' pool?"

The young woman set a hand lightly on Shironne's shoulder to let her know where she stood. "Miss Anjir?"

Cerradine watched her escort the girl out of the office, and then picked up his own hat. "What do you really think, David?"

Aldassa shifted in his chair. "I think we need to step back, sir."

Cerradine felt his brows rise. "Are you suggesting we drop the investigation?"

"No, sir," Aldassa said, "but we've been thinking of this scene primarily as Lieutenant Kassannan's murder. Personal for all of us, so we haven't been looking at the whole scene. Focusing on one player instead."

Aldassa's wife sometimes sewed costumes for a local theater, so the analogy made sense. It was an apt one. If he backed away from Hanna's death, he had one officer slipping away from her partner, apparently so that she could trail him. That had ended in either Jonnada or the police officer shooting her and then hiding her murder by blowing up part of a building, possibly with the collusion of someone who worked there.

"So, the question becomes why was Hanna following Jonnada?" Surely this had something to do with imports. A great deal of the country's needs were imported, paid for in gold or traded in exchange for wool and mutton and beef and, on occasion, ice. Larossa imported spices by the wagon load, and tea and silk and cotton. And there was the trade in drugs...one of the generals had asked his office to investigate it to reduce the number of soldiers entrapped by opium. "They were just looking into the illicit import-export issue, I thought."

"Yes, sir. Also, why kill her? And why go so far to hide her murder?"

"If they'd simply left her lying in the street, there would have been an investigation. They wanted to avoid one."

"Enough so to destroy part of a factory, sir?" Aldassa sat with his lips pressed together. "Don't think a drug dealer would go to that much trouble. Pay off a few people and he'd stay out of prison."

"Then we'll keep our eyes open for something bigger behind it." Cerradine decided to leave the pursuit in Aldassa's capable hands for the evening. Aldassa would probably sit here for a few hours, his clever mind ticking away at every bit of evidence. "I'm going to go talk to Kassannan again," he told Aldassa. "Maybe Hanna said something to him about Jonnada that will fill out our scene."

Unfortunately, Cerradine didn't find anyone at Aron Kassannan's flat.

* * *

Shironne woke in the middle of the night. Her heart beat fast, fear still prickling along her arms. Somewhere out in the city, someone lay newly dead. The Angel of Death had dreamed again and made her share that dream. It had been a *fast* death this time, a bullet and a sudden end.

The house remained silent, even the crickets quiet at this hour. She reached over to her nightstand, clutched her focus, and took a calming breath. Her mind clamored that she should get up and do something, but there was no chance her mother would let her report in at this hour, so she rolled over and tried to sleep again.

Later, she sat in the kitchens after breakfast, listening to her youngest sister read while she waited, rather impatiently. Her head hurt a bit, likely from a poor night's sleep. The appearance of Ensign Navinne at the servant's door relieved her. *Finally!*

With her mother's reluctant permission, Shironne accompanied the ensign to a coach waiting in the alleyway behind the house's mews. The colonel sat within, his impatience more marked than her own. "I'm not sure what you *can* do, Miss Anjir, but I need any help you can give us, and quickly."

He was far more agitated than Shironne had seen him

before. "Someone did die last night, didn't they?"

"Yes. Our missing Lieutenant Jonnada."

The guarded sound to Cerradine's voice made Shironne expect more, though. "And?"

"The police have arrested Captain Kassannan for his murder."

Surprise made her mouth fall open. "What? You don't think he did it, do you?"

"No, of course not," Cerradine said, his mind scoffing at the idea. "Jonnada was found dead at his brother's flat this morning, and Kassannan was there. Only circumstantial. I went down to the jail to talk to Kassannan myself. He wanted to question Jonnada, so he trailed the man to his brother's flat. But after Jonnada went inside, Kassannan heard a gunshot. He went inside to look for Jonnada, and found him dead. That's when the police showed up. Poor timing. They consider Kassannan's presence at the scene sufficient cause to hold him for both the murder of Jonnada and his wife."

That was *all* wrong. She could feel the colonel's anger, echoing her own frustration. "But Lieutenant Aldassa told me the captain was at *his* flat the night his wife was killed."

"I know. The police say they have a credible witness who claims he saw Kassannan at the scene of his wife's murder.

Aldassa's word against another man's. They haven't divulged whose, though."

"What about Aldassa's wife?" Shironne asked. "Surely she must have seen the captain there."

The colonel's irritation flared about him. "The authorities claim that a wife's not a credible witness. She would say whatever her husband told her to."

Shironne realized she was grinding her teeth together, and forced herself to stop. That was her own frustration, not the colonel's. "That's not fair," she protested. She could sense Navinne's silent agreement.

Cerradine seemed resigned. "It doesn't matter whether it's fair. We're fighting to get Aron released to the army, but that might take days. We need to figure out what's going on *now*, so you'd better tell me about your dream."

As they drove to the army's headquarters, Shironne related the scattered bits of the dream. It had been a flash of fear, and then a quick end—the shortest dream she'd ever shared with the Angel of Death. There hadn't been much time to form impressions of the situation.

She felt the colonel's frustration spreading about him like a pool of water. "Very well," the colonel said when she'd reached the end. "Are you up to viewing the body?"

Shironne nodded. "I want to find out who killed Lieutenant Kassannan, sir. Even if Lieutenant Jonnada didn't do it, he might have known who did."

"And I suspect he's dead because of it.

* * *

Lieutenant Farhana hadn't formally met Shironne before, and Cerradine decided it would be best to keep it that way. Farhana would complain to everyone who'd listen about her presence in the morgue, and Cerradine didn't want her name spread about. His own personnel were circumspect, but Farhana didn't answer to him.

The lieutenant scowled when they entered the morgue, even without seeing Shironne's face. She walked down the steps to the morgue, her scarf pulled over her face, and waited at the bottom of the steps. She wore a pink tunic today, with orange petticoats and a gold scarf that matched the embroidery on her clothes. Although the garments were worn with age, the embroidery on them had once been very fine. It was easy to guess that she was of the upper class, and clearly *not* one of

Cerradine's staff.

He gestured at the door. "Lieutenant, you can leave now."

"A lady should not be unchaperoned down here, sir," Farhana said, eyes flicking between them.

"In the morgue? Are you concerned that our dead lieutenant might accost her? Or perhaps you're implying that I would?"

"No, sir. Of course not, sir," Farhana backpedaled, dark face flushing. "Sorry, sir."

"Just go, Lieutenant."

Farhana bustled past them and out to the stairwell that led to the ground floor of the hospital.

"He's more concerned about the rules than his patients," Cerradine admitted after the door swung shut. He went to Shironne's side and raised her hand to his arm. "Come with me."

The mortuary service had already taken Hanna Kassannan's body away to prepare it for burial. A new body lay on the table, though. Cerradine pulled back the sheets, revealing the body of a young man whose brown skin had faded in death.

Shironne stripped off her glove, tucked it into her pocket, and reached out. Her hand came to rest on a linen-covered arm. She lifted her hand and moved it upward, tapping gingerly until she located his face. Then she pressed her hand against his skin, as if trying to reach farther than skin-deep.

Cerradine waited for a moment, expecting her to tell him what she'd found. Only she didn't. She simply stood there unmoving, her hand on Lieutenant Jonnada's cold temple.

* * *

Shironne pressed her skin against the dead man's, feeling the blood separating, the cooling—all the imbalances that lead to putrefaction building in the body.

Thoughts still resided there. Unlike Hanna Kassannan's disordered and broken mind, this one had things where they should be, far easier for Shironne to understand, lying like dead leaves in piles. She began to shift them, hunting the right thoughts, the ones that would tell her who had killed this man, and why Hanna Kassannan had died.

Many of the leaves told her of shame. He'd made a terrible mistake and couldn't think of any way to right it. She found a leaf that told her he'd felt he deserved to die, the saddest thing. That, at the end, he deserved to have a bullet in him. He'd gone too far and cost Hanna's life. *Guilt*.

She dug deeper, seeking the night of the hunt in Jonnada's

memories. She almost missed it. When she did, the perspective was all wrong. He hadn't been next to Kassannan, he'd been at the end of that alleyway. She had been following him, only he'd believed he'd evaded her. Shironne dug into those memories, seeking names and relationships.

Once she'd found enough, she pulled her hand away

She immediately felt the colonel's concern all about her like a warm blanket. The strength of her physical contact with the body had drowned it out before. She couldn't touch her focus in her pocket to help push it away—her hands were too dirty. "Um, sir...I think I've found what you need."

His worry subsided into relief, an emotion much easier for her to bear. "Do you realize how long that took? I was thinking about pulling you away."

Ah, that's what troubled him. "I'm sorry, sir, I didn't mean to worry you."

"You were at it for almost half an hour."

Still holding her hand away from her clothes, Shironne tried to decide if that sounded right. Sometimes it took longer, particularly if a body was fresh, the memories still clear in the victim's mind. "There was a lot to sort through, sir."

The colonel made a dry laughing sound, or perhaps it was

a choking sound. He reined in his worry, though. "What did you learn?"

"There was a policeman, and the mill owner."

His attention fixed on her fiercely. "Names?"

She picked through the box of Jonnada's memories she held in her mind. "The policeman is named Ranjan and the mill owner is Pallav, the smelly man who was in the alley yesterday. Jonnada was supposed to meet Pallav and Ranjan behind the mill to make some arrangement about a schedule. There was a shipment coming in, and Pallav wanted to assure that his buyers would be safe coming to look it over. Ranjan and Jonnada were meeting there to reassure Pallav that the police and the army wouldn't find out when the meeting was planned."

The colonel seemed concerned, but kept his voice level. "And what happened?"

"Jonnada thought he'd lost Kassannan. Intentionally, I mean. He came all the way back to the office here to make it seem the other way, like she'd slipped away. Then he went out to his meeting. Kassannan must have been following him the whole time. Jonnada met with Pallav to tell him the army didn't know anything, but Ranjan came up the alley late, and surprised Kassannan. She shot him—just in the arm. Jonnada remembered pointing at her, that's all, and Pallav shot her in the back. Jonnada was horribly upset about Kassannan, and afraid for his brother. It had all gone wrong."

"His brother? Whose brother?"

She'd failed to explain that part. "Jonnada's. That was the beginning. Pallav knew Jonnada's brother; he was his supplier. Pallav told Jonnada he had to help with the meeting, or he would hurt his brother. That's why Jonnada did all of this. To protect his younger brother."

The colonel's anger and disappointment seeped past his control for a moment, but then he carefully drew them back in. "If there was a problem, he should have brought it to me, but we've had...difficulties in the past. Did Jonnada see who ambushed him?"

"Yes, sir. It was the policeman, Ranjan."

"And that explains why the police arrived so quickly. I wonder if Ranjan might be our so-called credible witness, as well."

She had no way to verify that from Jonnada's memories, not when it happened after his death.

The colonel's mind spun down into thought, hiding away from her. Then his attention returned to her, sharp and determined. "What meeting was so important that Pallav was paying a police officer and blackmailing an army officer to protect it? Did Jonnada know?"

"Jonnada wasn't sure. He was...very unhappy about being trapped into helping, and he was telling himself he didn't *want* to know. That he just had to get through the deal and then get his brother out of the city. He wanted to run away, never to hurt anyone."

Grim anger settled around the colonel. She thought he'd been angry with Jonnada before, but now he felt sympathy for the man. "Where was Jonnada's brother all this time?" he asked.

"Jonnada couldn't find him. He went to check his brother's flat one last time before he fled the city."

"And that's where the policeman ambushed him." Cerradine's mind clicked away like a clock as he plotted and weighed possibilities. Then he said, "I have a plan. Are you willing to play along?"

* * *

It took some time to have everything ready. "Do you understand what we want?" Cerradine asked Shironne again.

She nodded her head. "Yes, sir. I'm here to listen."

"You are to keep your face covered at all times," he added. If Pallav had the nerve to threaten an army lieutenant's brother, then he didn't want the man to have any idea of Shironne's identity. That was the main flaw in this plan—it put Shironne at risk.

"Yes, sir." Her tone sounded aggrieved, as if his worry had started to annoy her.

Navinne sat next to Shironne, assigned to record the interview. After a moment, Lieutenant Aldassa opened the door, the mill owner with him. Cerradine caught a whiff of smoke on the man, a sickly-sweet scent he recognized, making him suspect that Pallav had taken refuge in some of his wares.

Aldassa made the man sit down at the table facing Cerradine, while Shironne and Navinne sat on the end. Cerradine waited until the man had settled. "Jonnada told us everything," he said calmly.

Pallav's sallow face took on a disbelieving look. "Who?"

"Now, the way I see it," Cerradine continued, "you're importing more than cotton thread from the coast. You need contacts to keep you out of trouble, the police, the military."

"More than cotton?"

"I can smell the opium on you," Cerradine said. "Not a serious offense in itself, but if the police were to determine that you were bringing in large quantities, they would have to pay attention. So, I need to know who brings it in, where you keep your supply and who sells it for you."

Pallav shifted in his seat, trying to make himself more of a presence, the attempt already spoiled by his slouching entry.

Cerradine gestured in Shironne's direction. "Madam, would you come sit across from this man?"

Navinne tapped Shironne on the back of her gloved hand. Shironne rose and, feeling the edge of the table, made her way to the empty chair. Cerradine placed her hand on the back of it. Shironne settled there gracefully, not giving a single hint that she was blind.

"This lady was able to find out what Jonnada knew," Cerradine said, "and now it's your turn."

Pallav's shrugged. "That's not possible. He's dead."

Cerradine noted he no longer denied knowing Jonnada. Perhaps the man was still under opium's cloud.

"He believes that," Shironne said.

Pallav gaped at her.

"Now," Cerradine said, "one question at a time. Did you

shoot Lieutenant Kassannan? Yes or no?"

The man took a second to reply. "No, of course not."

"He's lying," Shironne said, no hint of doubt in her voice. Pallav's eyes jerked toward her veiled face, fear unmistakable in his eyes this time.

"Did you shoot Lieutenant Jonnada?" Cerradine asked.

"No," Pallav protested.

"That's the truth," Shironne said. Her head tilted as if she wanted to hear him better.

Pallav hissed, his face growing paler. "Is she a priest?"

Apparently, the man feared the church more than the army. Cerradine ignored that. "Did you instruct Officer Ranjan to shoot Lieutenant Jonnada?"

"No," the man said slowly.

Shironne shook her veiled head. "I couldn't tell that time, sir."

"Did you instruct Ranjan to kill Lieutenant Jonnada?" Cerradine repeated.

"No!" Pallav tried to rise, but Aldassa put a hand on the man's shoulder and slammed him back into his seat.

"A lie, sir." Shironne held up her gloved hand for a moment. "He's trying to think his way around it because he knows I'm a sensitive. It was the word *shoot*. He probably never used exactly that word, but when you changed it to *kill*, then it became an outright lie."

"I want out of here!" Pallav yelled.

"Not until we have the answers to our questions," Cerradine said.

Shironne spoke before he got to the next one. "Sir, if I were to touch him, you wouldn't have to ask. I could just find the answers in his mind. It would be easier if he were dead, though," she added.

Whatever the man thought she meant by that, it provoked a profound reaction in him. He began shaking. Surprising them all, Pallav jumped up and grabbed at her, whether to hurt her or beg her for mercy, Cerradine didn't know. He yanked Shironne out of the man's reach as Aldassa and Navinne wrestled Pallav down to the table. Aldassa held the man down, his weight pinning the man. Pallav cried out in pain.

Navinne had used the closest weapon at hand; she'd jammed her pen into the back of the man's hand.

Shironne stood with her back against wall, her scarf fortunately still veiling her face. Her breath came fast, whether in reaction to their agitation or her own, Cerradine didn't know.

She grasped her focus in one gloved hand.

"Don't try that again," Navinne told the prisoner in a cold voice.

Cerradine tried to dampen his fury, not wanting to bother Shironne. "He lays a hand on her again, lieutenant, I want you to put that pen into his eyeball, not his hand. Understand?"

"Yes, sir," Navinne said angrily. "Absolutely, sir."

The mill owner whimpered. Aldassa got him back in his chair, this time securing his arms behind him. No more pretense of a friendly discussion.

"Sir," Shironne said softly. "I know why he's so afraid."

Cerradine glanced at her, chilled. The man *had* gotten a hand on her. Even though fabric, Shironne could pick things up. "What is it?"

"Can I...can I speak to you in the hallway?"

Cerradine put a hand under her elbow and led her out of the interrogation room. When he'd closed the door, he turned back to her. "What is it, Miss Anjir? He touched you, didn't he?"

She pulled off her scarf held it crumpled to her chest. With one hand, she fumbled for the focus in her pocket, probably using the thing to calm herself. Her face looked nearly as pale as the mill owner's. "He wanted to beg me, sir, not to tell."

"You could tell that when he touched you?"

She nodded her head jerkily. "But there was more. He's not just selling drugs, sir. Um, he brings them in from the countryside and sells them."

He had never seen her quite so upset. "Sells what?"

Her lips quivered. "Um, girls, sir. Like me, younger. Sometimes boys," she finished on a whisper.

He regretted letting Pallav get anywhere near her now. He'd rather not have her know such a trade occurred in a civilized city. "So, that's what he was afraid you would find out."

"Not that, sir." She took a deep breath, and then seemed calmer. "It's *who* he works for, sir, not that he sells...things. He works for important people, and he thinks they'll kill him to keep him quiet."

That explained bringing in a police officer and a soldier. "Important people?"

"Like in the police....and um, politicians."

Politicians. She hadn't said it aloud, as if keeping it inside her head would keep it from being true. *Her father.*

His stomach felt hollow. He'd always been aware this *might* happen, that she would be involved in an investigation that touched on her father's less savory dealings. He'd hoped not, though. And he hadn't known her father was involved in something as low as the trade in human flesh. "I'm so sorry, Shironne."

"He's very afraid of my father," she whispered. "And my father's friends."

For a full minute, Cerradine actually contemplated asking her if she would try to get more information out of the man. She *could* do that. She could give them all the details Pallav knew.

He looked down at her delicate face. A tear ran down one cheek. He leaned back toward the interrogation room, opened the door a crack and called for Navinne. The ensign emerged a second later. "Will you take Miss Anjir to my office, Ensign? Perhaps get her something to drink as well?"

Navinne shot a glance at Shironne's distraught face and nodded briskly. "Yes, sir. Of course, sir."

She led Shironne away.

* * *

When Cerradine joined her a short while later, Shironne looked calmer. "I knew," she said quietly as he entered. "I mean, I know my father's not a good man."

He'd known that too, but hadn't known about her father's more objectionable business ventures. He couldn't forget that knowledge now, nor could he make her do so. He sat down on the edge of the desk and considered her gravely for a moment. "Because the deaths of two army personnel are involved, we can prosecute Pallav and Ranjan. The army doesn't have the authority to prosecute anything else, though. Anything not directly pertaining to the deaths of our officers will have to be turned over to the police to handle."

"Oh," she said softly.

Her father was a crony of the police commissioner, and it was likely that if Anjir was involved in this business, Commissioner Faralis would ignore the charges. Cerradine didn't have the leverage to force the man do his job.

Shironne bit at her lip, likely catching his frustration. "At least now we know why Lieutenant Kassannan died."

"She must have suspected Jonnada's involvement," he said. "I wish she had brought her suspicions to me. Or that Jonnada would have come to us to protect his brother."

"But you can't change the past, sir," she said. "They'll let Captain Kassannan out of jail now, won't they?"

That was something he *could* fix. "As soon as I get you home,

Miss Anjir, I'm going to the jail myself. I'll pry him out if I have to."

That brought a fleeting smile to her face. "Good."

* * *

Hours later, he stood in the kitchen in the Anjir house, waiting with Shironne for her mother to come down. She was avoiding her own butler, he knew. The man regularly reported her movements back to her husband.

Aron Kassannan was back at his own flat, the other inhabitants of that building keeping an eye on him. They didn't want to leave him alone again. They'd run down Officer Ranjan, and he and Pallav now waiting in cells for the military lawyers to question them further about the murders.

Now there was one last tricky bit to handle—breaking the news of impending scandal to Shironne's mother, who would not be pleased. Savelle Anjir hated scandal more than anything.

When she came down the steps into the kitchen, Savelle Anjir glanced between her daughter and him, lovely eyes worried. "Why are you in my house? He's sure to hear of this."

The cook, a large woman who was very protective of Savelle

Anjir, moved to block the servant's stair, her eyes turned upward as she kept watch.

"It's necessary this time," he told her. "I've passed the information we had to the police, and you need to know that one of the culprits implicated your husband."

Savelle Anjir nodded once, chin raised. "Shironne told me. The police will simply bury this, Colonel, as they do every hint of my husband's deeds."

"Not this time," he warned. "Not completely."

She glanced to the cook for reassurance and turned back to him. "What do you mean?"

"There's a third party involved now," he said, "a writer for one of the newspapers. They have promised to publish the things that I cannot prosecute. And a priest came to witness the handoff."

Shironne's head turned in his direction, her mouth dropping open. He'd managed to surprise her. The priest would be safe in his temple, but Cerradine had needed to pull strings to guarantee the writer's safety and his publisher's. He was willing to hire bodyguards out of his own pocket if he must.

Savelle Anjir gripped the edge of the table with one slender hand, her bracelet tinkling. "They will..."

Once it hit the newspapers, the church would pursue this doggedly. Even though they had no power to prosecute crimes, they had *influence*. They had the will of the people behind them, and could darken the reputation of anyone who crossed them.

"My husband will..." She took a shallow breath and tried again. "You said you wouldn't...*interfere* in our family. You promised."

He had, more or less. When Shironne had come to work for him, Cerradine had told Savelle he would do his best not to expose *her* to gossip by exposing her husband's misdeeds. But then he'd thought it merely blackmail, keeping mistresses, and gambling—the sort of thing one expected of politicians. "This is about children being sold into slavery," he said softly. "Do you believe that should be allowed to continue?"

"No, of course not," she whispered, crumpling her scarf between her hands.

"May I suggest again that you go to your brothers, Madam? They will protect you."

The look she gave him suggested dry exasperation. Not for the first time, Cerradine wished he was a sensitive so he could tell what she was feeling.

"I do not need *their* interference either, Colonel." She took a deep breath and lifted her chin. "What will happen to him?"

"That I cannot guarantee. He will be put under a great deal of pressure. The police will find someone to blame once the extent of this comes out."

"They will all turn on each other," she said softly.

"Yes," Cerradine said. "I'd like to place a couple of officers in your household. They will be here primarily to protect you and the girls. They will have orders to keep your husband out of this house."

Legally, he had no right to do that. Legally, her husband could do whatever he wanted to her and her daughters. But in truth, Cerradine *could* protect her and her family.

"People will talk," she said in half a whisper.

"Shironne has told me you no longer have a maid," he said, "so one of the women in the office has volunteered to take that job. And Messine has said he'll take over your mews. You'll simply appear to have hired a couple of new servants."

"Mama," Shironne said, "you should agree."

The cook added her gruff agreement. Cerradine held his mouth grimly shut. Even Savelle Anjir couldn't turn his offer down gracefully now.

She lifted her chin. "I will not say no, then, Colonel."

"Good." Cerradine couldn't stop the firestorm of gossip that would soon descend on Madam Anjir's head, but he could protect her from her husband's possible reprisals once the man learned that Shironne had a part in his downfall. This was one of the things he *could* fix. "Now, I had best leave before my coming is noticed."

Savelle Anjir reached over and laid her slender hand atop his, something he didn't think she'd ever done before. "Thank you, Colonel. I am grateful for your consideration."

He wasn't sure whether she meant his arranging for guards, or his quick departure, but he wasn't going to question it. "You're most welcome, Madam. Good night, Shironne."

It was the beginning of the end for that family. He could only hope there would be a new beginning for them once the smoke cleared. He would do his best to see that it was so.

THE END

To read more about Shironne and Mikael, turn the page to read the first two chapters of the novel, *Dreaming Death*.

Praise for J. Kathleen Cheney's
Dreaming Death

"Cheney is very good at sensory detail, especially blind Shironne's perceptions as she begins exploring Mikael's world."—*Publishers Weekly*

"*Dreaming Death* is a book of mystery, magic, and overwhelming potential which promises more good things to come from J. Kathleen Cheney."—*The Speculative Herald*

"This imaginative new fantasy world is based on a tasty mixture of psychic talents and deadly magic."—*Kirkus, February's Speculative Fiction You Can't Miss*

* * *

Excerpt from Dreaming Death

Chapter 1

Liran Prifata's dove-gray uniform jacket lay to one side, his shirt tangled with it, pale blotches on the bare dirt. The rain pelted down, and the wind in the picked-over field tore at him. He was chilled to the bone, too numb to fight any longer.

Two of the men grasped his arms, pinning him on his knees like an animal to be slaughtered. The rain softened the ground into a muddy quagmire. Blood mixed with the water dripping from his chest, staining his trousers, all color leached out in the dark. A third man in a dark jacket leaned over him, light glinting off a curved knife as he sliced, and cut again. Liran felt no pain, but the numbness scared him more than being captive. He wanted to scream, cry out for help. His throat wouldn't answer. His lungs could hardly find the air to breathe, much less cry out.

What are they doing to me?

The man in the dark jacket spoke as he worked, words that meant nothing in Liran's ears. He'd heard no names, seen nothing unusual about their clothes, no marks on the coach that would help his fellow police identify these men. The men didn't even hide their faces from him, but they had neither marks nor scars to distinguish them in his mind.

This had to be blood magic. He'd never seen it before, but there was no other name for what they were doing, letting his blood fall onto the earth. The Pedraisi did this in their fields, some ancient fertility right. It was illegal, and forbidden by the temple. *God won't permit this*, he told himself. *Not here in Noikinos. He will send someone to save me.*

His tormenter stepped back and held up a lantern to survey his handiwork. Another man, the fourth one Liran had seen in the coach, came closer. Liran tried to focus on that face, to sear it into his memory, but he couldn't make out the man's features, hidden beneath the hat the man wore to stave off the cold rain. A fifth man huddled in the distance, face turned away as if he was ashamed.

Now that he'd bled for them, for their magic, surely they would let him go. They would leave him here, and someone would find him. The farmer would come to find out who had desecrated his wheat field to appease a false god.

The fourth man gestured sharply, and the man with the knife came close again. He made a single sharp movement, the blade slashing across this time, a flash in the darkness.

That hurt. Enough to reach through the numbness, enough to tell Liran it was no shallow cut like the others. He gasped feebly, and then he was falling. He landed on his side in the shorn remains of the field's wheat. Feet squelched away in the muck.

Darkness gathered in the edges of Liran's vision. *Why me?*

Warmth gathered in his soul, belying the dark and cold. He had the sense of a presence like hands resting on his shoulders. An angel had come to take him to the promised heavens.

Chapter 2

Shironne stood on the balcony outside her room, wishing the wind could sweep the night's tattered images from her mind. The dream haunted her. Down in the city, someone had died.

She clutched her heavy robe about her, grateful for its warmth. Winter had come early to Noikinos. The chilly wind carried up with it the damp and earthy scent of the mews behind the house, the smells of horse and hay and manure.

Dry leaves rattled and sighed in the crisp breeze. The trees planted along the side of the house would cling to them until spring when the softer whisper of new leaves would replace the rusty winter sound. When she'd been able to see, she'd thought the brown leaves unattractive. Now that she was blind, she listened to them instead, their rustle providing a clear demarcation of the edge of her family's property. Somewhere nearby pennants snapped and chimes tinkled, although she couldn't tell which neighbor had brought those from the temple to safeguard their home.

The cook spoke with a tradesman in the back courtyard, the clink of metal and glass underlying their voices, and echoing off the stone walls of the back courtyard. Likely the milkman, Shironne decided. The distant noise of carriages and horses spoke of morning traffic—sounds of normalcy.

No one knows yet—no one but me and him. It had been one of *those* dreams.

At first, she hadn't known they weren't her own.

There was a man up at the palace who dreamed of death, deaths that were really happening. He involuntarily spun out those dreams, sharing the victim's fear and pain with the world. For most who could sense his dreams, that meant little more than a vague sense of fear and an occasional headache.

As in everything else, I have to be the one who's different.

Colonel Cerradine knew who the dreamer was, this man who inflicted his nightmares on her. The colonel had always refused to tell her anything about him, though, not even his name. Lacking any better label for him, Shironne had settled on the Angel of Death, a nickname the colonel's personnel seemed to find both apt...and ridiculous.

She rubbed one hand with the other, her right thumb smoothing along the scar that ran across her left palm. The souvenir of a foolish childhood accident, it served as a constant reminder that she too often let curiosity get the better of her.

But every time she woke from one of these dreams, she wondered about him. *Who is he? Why does he do this?*

The colonel had warned her that pushing to find that answer too soon could be dangerous for her. What he hadn't told her was *why*. What harm could there be in meeting someone whose dreams she already shared? After all, those shared dreams, however unpleasant, had given rise to her unusual vocation.

The angel's dreams gave her a purpose beyond simply finding a husband...or joining the priesthood, as was expected of Larossans who developed powers. When her powers had abruptly manifested when she was twelve, the chance of finding a husband had disappeared. Shironne had to consider other paths, but the priesthood didn't seem appealing either, selling charms and prayers in the temple wouldn't suit her temperament at all, she'd insisted. That infuriated her father and shocked the priests who'd more than once come to talk to her mother about it. After all, they asked, what else is a girl child to do with her life?

Shironne was terribly grateful that her mother supported her decision to find another path, and that those dreams had shown her one. Those dreams always meant there was death, and she could do something about them. She could help find murderers.

Thus had begun her strange career with the army.

The man who dreamed often couldn't remember much about them. She *could*. That had seemed odd at first. Then she'd grasped that his dreams were like a painting laid before her in her sleep, but the Angel of Death didn't see them that way. Instead, his mind was the canvas on which they were painted.

She stepped back inside her bedroom, closed the door after her, and drew the curtain shut. Not certain how long she'd stood on the balcony savoring the breeze, she crossed to the mantel and carefully felt the delicate hands of the clock. Her mother had removed the glass bezel, making it possible for Shironne to read the time with her fingers. It was almost eight.

Her bedroom door opened, and Melanna pelted into the room, bare feet slapping against the wooden floor. Melanna's steps came toward her, her bracelet tinkling, and then her arms clasped about Shironne's waist in a fierce hug. The top of Melanna's head almost reached Shironne's shoulder. Her youngest sister was on her way to being as tall as their mother one day, if not taller.

"I had bad dreams," Melanna complained, quickly turning her loose.

Shironne set a bare hand atop her sister's coarse hair—a

trait certainly not inherited from their mother. Whenever she touched another person, she could feel more than their emotions. She could actually feel the thoughts buzzing around in their heads like a swarm of bees, sometimes formed into words she could catch, other times not. She found only a vague sense of Melanna's nightmare, but the girl rarely remembered anything specific from the angel's dreams. Their mother didn't either.

Even Shironne's memories of the dreams were unclear, as if she'd seen everything through a heavy veil. She knew she'd witnessed a murder. It was *always* murder, even if it didn't seem that way at first. The faceless victim hadn't been able to fight back, and his captors—there had been more than one, of that Shironne was sure—had cut his skin. Then they'd let him die. It had been cold and raining, somewhere near the river. A field, perhaps, although she wasn't sure why she'd drawn that conclusion. But each detail might help the army find a murderer, or murderers in this case, so she needed to report them.

"I have to find my gloves," she told her sister. "Then we can go down for breakfast."

"Can we read first?" Melanna asked.

Her youngest sister had acquired a lurid novel from a

lending library that was *their* secret. It wasn't one her governess, Verinne, would find acceptable. The book was full of Pedraisi witchcraft. It had witches who made stables go up in flames and others who could call birds from the air. Larossans possessed a variety of powers, but those were pure nonsense. Even so, they made for an entertaining tale. The story also had an unlikely romance between the heroine and a handsome young Larossan man who worked in her father's stables, whom Shironne strongly suspected would turn out to be the missing son of a lord or wealthy landowner.

Melanna did most of the reading, but would spell out the longer words so that Shironne could tell her how to pronounce them. "Not now," Shironne said. "When Verinne takes her nap you can come to my room."

Melanna huffed out a dramatic sigh and slipped away from Shironne's grasp. A second later, Shironne heard her sister bound onto her mattress. Shironne returned to her bed and sat, locating her gloves on the table next to her bed just where she'd left them. While Shironne tugged on the gloves, Melanna continued to jump on the bed, one particularly large bounce telling Shironne her sister had flopped onto her back.

Shironne reached out to the table again and found her

focus. Pure quartz, she could trace along the perfect lines within the stone, even through her gloves. She'd used this stone as a focus for some time now and was as familiar with it as she was with her worn clothes. It was still endlessly fascinating. When she concentrated on it all the other sensations that assailed her faded away: the feel of fabric against her skin, the hints of smoke on the air that brushed her face, the lingering traces of the last item she'd touched. She could shut out the constant barrage of others' emotions and simply follow the emotionless lines of the stone, clearing the clutter from her mind.

She concentrated on it a moment longer, chasing away the dragging grip of last night's dream. Then she pulled her attention back. "Are you ready to go down?" she asked her sister.

Melanna promptly clambered off the bed, and together they headed downstairs to the kitchens. It wasn't proper for them to eat in the kitchen, but they did so anyway, since Cook was nearly a part of the family, having come from their mother's childhood home with her.

Pausing at the base of the kitchen stairs, Shironne heard the customary oofing sound Cook made when Melanna ran to hug her. Then came the scrape of the bench when Melanna sat down at the table. The room smelled of baking flatbread and spices. Shironne went to join her sister, pulled out the chair at the head of the table, and settled there.

"Is Kirya around?" she asked Cook. Kirya Aldrine was actually an army lieutenant the colonel had placed within their household to assure the family's safety, but the young woman spent most of her days working as maid for Shironne's mother and the elder of her sisters, Perrin.

Since Mama was in mourning, her garb wasn't complicated. Until a year had passed, her tunic, trousers, and petticoats would all be of undyed silk and wool. She didn't wear any jewelry save for the bracelet that helped Shironne hear where she was. That made Kirya's assignment as maid easier. Perrin, on the other hand, was to be presented to the elite of Larossan society at the turn of the year in the hope of contracting a brilliant marriage. She got to wear bright colors, the cuffs and hems of her tunics and petticoats heavily embroidered, and Mama had given Perrin the jewelry she no longer wore. Working on Perrin's wardrobe *did* keep Kirya busy.

Cook's worry spun about her at the mention of Kirya. "I think she's up with your mother. Should I send for her?"

Shironne realized that Cook must think something was wrong. "No. What about Messine?"

Filip Messine, another lieutenant, primarily watched over Shironne. He escorted her to her various assignments for the army. In his false identity here, though, he served as a groom in the mostly empty stable. The Anjir family had limited funds at the moment, so there were only the two old carriage horses there. They could spare Messine for an errand or two.

Cook's worry faded to relief. "Oh, you want a messenger. I'll go call him." She walked to the outside door and called out into the courtyard before returning to her cooking.

A moment later, Shironne heard the door open again, followed by the jangle of bells and Messine's familiar footsteps. Shironne turned her head that way to hear him better. Although she could *sense* where the members of their little household were when she concentrated, the various bracelets and bells each wore made it easier for her to locate them.

Messine came closer, clutching his concern tight about him. He was trained not to bother others with his emotions. For Shironne, that made him pleasing company. "Miss Anjir, did you need me?"

"I need to send a message to the colonel," she explained. "I had a dream. Someone died, and the Angel of Death dreamed it."

END OF EXCERPT

If you're interested in reading more about Shironne and Mikael's quest to find the killer, you will find it in *Dreaming Death*, available at booksellers everywhere.

About the Author:

J. Kathleen Cheney taught mathematics ranging from 7th grade to Calculus, but gave it all up for a chance to write stories. Her novella "Iron Shoes" was a 2010 Nebula Award Finalist. Her novel, **The Golden City** was a Finalist for the 2014 Locus Awards (Best First Novel). **Dreaming Death** (Feb 2016) is the first in a new series, the *Palace of Dreams Novels*.

Other works by J. Kathleen Cheney

The Golden City Series
The Golden City
The Seat of Magic
The Shores of Spain
The Seer's Choice
After the War

Palace of Dreams Series
Dreaming Death
In Dreaming Bound (coming 2018)
Shared Dreams

The Books of The Horn
Oathbreaker, Original and Overseer

The King's Daughter Series
(coming 2018)
The Amiestrin Gambit
The Passing of Pawns
The Black Queen

Other Works
Iron Shoes: Tales from Hawk's Folly Farm
The Dragon's Child: Six Short Stories
Whatever Else
Fleurs du Mal
A Hand for Each
The Stains of the Past
The Bear Girl

For more info on any of these books, please visit www.jkathleencheney.com.

A Dream Palace Press Book

Made in United States
North Haven, CT
28 March 2022